The first message the shabby man had brought was simple . . .

"Lay off trying to find Stiff the Snow Man, or you'll be in big trouble."

Now the shabby man was back, his face scraped, his lower lip split and swollen, his left arm dangling uselessly by his side.

"They said I should deliver a second message," he whimpered. "Then they beat me up, drove me here and threw me out. But they never said what the second message was."

That told Nathan Phillips all he needed to know. The battered messenger *was* the second message - a brutal threat of violence to come!

To Lynn Anne,
a star teacher,
from her most loving pupil.

APRIL SNOW

Nick O'Donohoe

PaperJacks LTD.

Markham, Ontario, Canada

PaperJacks LTD.

One of a series of books
published by PaperJacks Ltd.

APRIL SNOW

PaperJacks edition published August 1984

Cover design: Croydon

Quotations from "Thirteen Ways of Looking at a Blackbird" and "The Snow
Man," copyright 1923 and renewed 1951, by Wallace Stevens. Reprinted from
The Collected Poems of Wallace Stevens by permission of the publisher, Alfred
A. Knopf, Inc.

This is a work of fiction in its entirety. Any resemblance to actual people, places
or events is purely coincidental.

ISBN 0-7701-0305-7
Copyright © 1981 by Nick O'Donohoe
Originally published in a limited edition by
Worldwide Library
All rights reserved
Printed in Canada

1

MILD APRIL DAYS in Minneapolis are too rare to spend in airport lobbies. I looked out the window of the main terminal, nearly going blind from the snow glare, and thought what a lot of fair weather and time I was wasting. I couldn't change the weather, though, and someone else was paying for my time; I closed my eyes and listened to the flight announcements and pagings. I could use the rest; I'd just come from a long funeral.

The PA speakers needed repair badly; every message was a mystery. "—Screw, Mrs. John Guru—" Really? Shame on you, Mrs. Guru. "—Banjo service nonstop to St. Petersburg—" God knows what they have to Nashville. "—Paging Mrs. Bagel, the Giant Kennedy passenger, Mrs. Bagel—"

One announcement turned everyone's head. As the same tired voice that had done the others began listlessly paging "the mother of Charles Guth," suddenly it was drowned out by a panic-stricken child shouting, "Hey, ma! Hey, ma! Hey, ma!" A few people stopped and laughed.

Immediately after that, more clearly than I'd expected, the PA said, "Mr. Phillips, Mr. Nathan Phillips, please come to the information booth." I made a swipe at my hair with one hand and walked up to the paging desk.

At the desk was a wheelchair. In it was a withered old lady in a faded brown dress. Her arms were thin, with tough, ropy muscles from years of pulling herself around. Her lips were thin, too—set in grim disappointment. They looked as though smiling would hurt. Her eyes were cold blue and caught the light disconcertingly. She wore no jewelry, even though I knew she could probably afford to have her wheelchair and attendant silvered. She spoke; her voice crackled like dry wood catching fire. "Mr. Phillips?"

I nodded. She didn't seem to want me to talk just yet. She looked at me carefully, thoroughly—as though she were guessing my height, weight and religion.

"I expected a much older man, Mr. Phillips. I was told your firm had been in business twenty years."

I had a feeling saying I was thirty-two might not impress her. "Actually, Mrs. Grey, it was my partner, Roy Cartley, who was in business that long. I've been a private investigator for five years."

"And where is Mr. Cartley this morning? I understood I was hiring an experienced detective."

I felt my jaw jump but only said, "Mr. Cartley died a few days ago in a car collision." She closed her eyes and said nothing. "And you are getting an experienced detective. I assume I came recommended. If you need more references, I took the precaution of typing up a list of them for you."

I handed her the sheet. She didn't look at it for more than five minutes, and no more carefully than a jeweler would check over the Star of India. She folded the list, put it in a side pocket of the wheelchair and said, to nobody in particular, "Very well." She turned to her attendant, a tall bronzed man in a gray suit. "You may go, Charles. Be here again in exactly forty minutes." He bowed briskly, turned on his heel and walked away. I hoped he had a stopwatch.

She turned to me. "Be so kind, Mr. Phillips, as to roll me through the terminal for a moment. I organize my thoughts better when I am in motion." I moved to the back of the chair, folding my coat over my arm. As I did, for the first time since I had seen her, something other than her head and arms moved. She raised herself up on her arms and shifted back in the chair as far as she could go. Her arms gripped the chair rests, braced for the shock of movement. The whole process looked acutely painful.

I moved the chair as gently as possible, leaning into it slightly and pulling back on the handles to make the start gradual. We rolled softly and silently past the information booth and the ticket counters.

After a minute or two she spoke. "You do this very well, Mr. Phillips. It's a pity that you are nothing but a nasty little man in a nasty little profession."

I looked down at her tightly pinned straight white hair for a moment before replying. "I may not have been in business all that long, Mrs. Grey, but I've noticed already that the people who say that to me are the ones who bring in the nastiest jobs. Somehow that never bothers them at all."

She sniffed. "I certainly don't see why your firm came recommended, unless Mr. Cartley was far superior to you. Your being his partner suggests he had no manners and very little sense."

I stopped the wheelchair. When I didn't say anything she snapped, "Well?"

I said slowly, "If it makes things any better I'll apologize for being rude. Suppose we leave my partner out of it; I'm a little touchy about him just now."

She turned her head to look at me; her neck cracked loudly, and she winced. "Young man, do

you want my business or don't you?'' I let that pass.
She turned back around and stared straight ahead.
"Unfortunately, I don't have time to quibble or
even to find another detective. I must get back to
Arizona and out of this wretched climate." She
looked bitterly out at the snow. I was surprised it
didn't melt. She sighed, a thin sound. "I'm sorry."

"Forget it. I'm sorry I was rude. What can I do for
you?"

We started rolling again, and she talked in a dull
mechanical voice. "I want you to find my son. To
the best of my knowledge, no one has seen him in
two years. My son consorted with unsavory charac-
ters; I'm sure you're acquainted with him and his
business."

I was tired of pushing her and more tired of her
attitude, but I kept the chair rolling and let that one
pass, too. "Just in case I don't know him, Mrs.
Grey, tell me your son's name. Maybe you have
more than one son."

She gripped the armrests and turned to look at me
again, this time pulling her whole torso with her.
Her face was furious; her mouth moved and nothing came out. When she could talk, her voice
screeched like a whetstone. "I have only one son,
Mr. Phillips. His birth nearly killed me. Since then I
have been in and out of health spas, hospitals and
wheelchairs. I tried for no more children. Even if
I'd tried, I could have had none." The final word
caught in her throat; she spat it out viciously, and a
spot of saliva fell from her lower lip and coursed
down her chin. She dabbed at it with a handkerchief she'd tucked in her right sleeve.

I cleared my throat, embarrassed. "Do you have a
picture of him, ma'am?" She fumbled in the pocket
of the left armrest and passed me up a newspaper
photograph of a man. He looked about thirty-five,

with light hair and eyes like his mother's. The clipping was dated a little over two years ago. The caption said, "Grey acquitted in Grogan murder."

I stared at it, then at her. "Steven Grey? Stiff the Snow Man?"

She nodded slowly and tiredly. "Yes. Steven Grey. Cocaine and heroin dealer, suspected murderer and gunman, suspected pimp, probable blackmailer. My son."

Sweat was beading up on my forehead. I pushed the wheelchair into a place in the sunlight and stopped. I pulled a chair over and sat across from her.

"Actually, Mrs. Grey, my par—my late partner and I assisted the D.A.'s office when your son was tried. We talked to a lot of witnesses and to his friends and, uh, business associates. The men he worked with aren't the gentlest people. Neither is your son."

She said sharply, "Does that mean you expect some kind of hazard pay?"

"My normal pay is hazard pay—seventy dollars a day, plus expenses. If that seems unreasonable, you'd better tell me now." She shook her head. "What it means is that I'll have some idea of where to start searching for your son—unless, of course, you have a better idea of where I should start."

She folded her hands and said with evident satisfaction, "Young man, I have no idea where Steven is. I have not seen him or spoken to him in more than ten years; I have not corresponded with him in five."

I turned the clipping over in my hands, looking at Grey's face. A hard face, even though it still had the smooth skin of a boy. "If that's so, how did you know he was missing?"

She craned her neck forward, then pulled her

body up to lean it toward me; she grimaced at the effort. "Steven sent me a check for one thousand dollars every month, without fail. The checks were never late, but two years ago they stopped coming. After a year I broke an old promise never to write him and sent a note asking what had happened. I received no reply, and the checks have not resumed. This is most unlike him; I feel sure that had my letters reached him he would have sent me a check, possibly even a note. I would have burned the note, of course."

That last bothered me. Maybe it was supposed to, but I couldn't let it go by. "Mrs. Grey, if you feel that way, why bother to look for your son? The checks are peanuts to you; we both know you could blow your nose on a thousand-dollar check and never know the difference. Why do you want his money so badly?"

She got mad again. She always would, about this. "It isn't his money. It's mine. It's owed me, all of it, for damages." She looked into my face. I must not have looked sympathetic. She clenched her knobbly fingers and snarled, "It's my *right*."

Her body was motionless but her arms were trembling; her voice cut through the lobby noise. Her fingers worked stiffly on the armrests like roots wrapping around boulders. People turned and looked, then hurried on their way. I wished I was hurrying with them.

She lowered her voice and said shakily, "Just find him. I don't care how long it takes, so long as you find him before I die. Find him, and tell him to start paying again."

I found my voice. "Sorry, I'm not Western Union. I'll tell you where he is, and you can do as you please with the information." She didn't like my tone but didn't argue; that surprised me.

I had one more thing to say, and I said it as gently as I could. Nasty, petty and vicious as she was, she was still that pitiable. "Mrs. Grey, I feel obliged to tell you that, given the business your son ran and the company he kept, there is a large chance that I'll discover he is dead."

She looked straight ahead, not at me or at anything else. Slowly, a tight, mad little smile creased her narrow, hollow-cheeked face. Then she winced. I had been right—smiling hurt.

Our forty minutes were nearly up. I rolled her back to the ticket counter; her uniformed man was there, still standing almost at attention, waiting for her. Maybe he was a former military man. Then again, maybe he was paid not to bend.

The material she gave me before she left was a quick summary of all she knew about her son in the past ten years. It wasn't much: a photostat of his signature, a copy of his last known address, a list of the checks he'd sent her up until two years ago and another photograph, this one from just after he graduated from college. All the information a concerned mother would need. I took it to the airport snack bar and stared at it during my lunch.

I thought about Elizabeth Grey all through the meal. I didn't like the chili, either.

2

AFTER LUNCH I went over to the headquarters of the Minneapolis Police, Homicide Division. I asked to see Lieutenant Jon Pederson. The desk sergeant, without looking up, told me to wait. I gave him my name and waited, reading the newspaper I hadn't read at the airport. The forecast was for partly cloudy skies and mild temperatures the next few days; the only person happier than me about that was the mailman.

The police radio came to life briefly to order a squad car to some address on Summit Avenue where a man was reported to have shot his wife. Two cars, both cruising near the Guthrie Theatre, answered immediately. I guess we all have our dull days.

Jon Pederson came to his door and motioned me into his office. Pederson was about fifty but barely graying, square jawed and Nordic looking in the way about a third of Minnesota is, and constantly irascible or unhappy, judging from his expression. Actually, he was even tempered, happy in his job and the best friend Roy Cartley ever had.

Pederson's office was a total litter of bulletins, reports, memos and personal notes. His desk was scarred—stained with old coffee spills, covered with cigarette burns and badly in need of replacement. So was most of his office furniture and machinery. He wouldn't let anyone requisition anything for him until its old counterpart had broken down; to him a new chair was a luxury. He never made an extra cent off his job and never wasted one, either.

He went behind his desk, fingered a pencil, poked at some papers with last month's date on them and said delicately, "So. How's business?"

"Not bad." I sat down and said, "How's your shoulder?"

He rubbed it. "Sore. I'll have a bruise tomorrow. Maybe I'm getting old to be a pallbearer."

"It's not age. I'm sore, too. Roy's brother leave okay?"

He nodded. "Jack caught the ten-thirty flight to L.A."

"Surprised I didn't see him at the airport." Jon looked puzzled, so I added, "Mrs. Elizabeth Grey flew in to see me this morning. Thanks."

He was pleased, then annoyed. "How did you know I recommended you for the job? Someone else could have; you must have friends somewhere."

I settled back in my chair. "More than you'd think." Only a few in Minneapolis, but why tell him that? "First, Elizabeth Grey had nothing to hide. She would have gone to the police for what she wanted, and when she found out that they weren't working on it, she would have asked them to recommend a private eye—provided, of course, she couldn't get God to recommend one. Now, since you're the only officer I know who would send her to me, it had to be you. Second, she knew how long Cartley's firm had been in business but didn't know I was a junior partner. Since anyone else would have told her the senior partner was dead, and no one else who wanted me to get the job would have avoided lying so neatly, I knew it was you. Third—"

"Okay, okay. It was me. As a matter of fact,

though, you're wrong about one thing: she didn't want any help from us. She didn't even ask about anything in particular, just said she was looking for a reputable P.I. and did we know one. I thought you might need the work till you get a reputation as a solo operator. I don't imagine you're finding things too busy right now."

I was having trouble finding things at all, but I didn't say so. He stopped pushing at the papers just before they reached the edge of the desk; he looked at me sharply. "Well? Aren't you going to thank me any better than that?" His ears turned red and he started playing with the pencils again.

I said, in as close to a growl as I could manage, "Actually, I was going to jump up and down and cry on your shoulder, but I thought I'd wait and see if I could still jump after I got a few bullets in me from your recommendation. Her business isn't my idea of a secure desk job."

"So. Who's got a secure desk job?" He gestured at his own paper-cluttered desk, barely visible under reports, bulletins and printouts. "I do more foot-work than the Russian ballet. Do you know how often I even get to see this desk?"

"The surface of it? I'd say never." He glared at me and began sorting papers into separate piles. The piles covered as much of the desk as the original clutter had. I said carefully, trying to sound casual, "I guess you know what she wants done."

He didn't look up. "She didn't want to discuss it with me." Pederson never lies, just gives the wrong truthful answers.

"I can't believe— No, strike that," I said hastily as he stopped dead. "I'm sure she didn't *want* to. But I'm just as sure whoever she talked to referred the call to you in case she was pulling something funny. And when somebody refers a lady named

Grey to you, after all the work you did on Stiff the
Snow Man's case, it doesn't take Solomon the Wise
to guess who she wants found." I pulled out a pencil, just to have something to do.

"This is the first I've heard of it," he said calmly,
picking up a clump of the papers he'd been shuf-
fling.

"Oh, she wrote you instead of calling, then?"

He slapped the papers down hard; several more
fell off one end of his desk. "Haven't you got anything better to do than call me a liar?" he barked.

We both grinned and quit fidgeting. I put the pencil back in my pocket. "As a matter of fact, Officer,
I do. I came here to ask if you have any information
you could tell me about Steven Grey—when he disappeared, who he was last seen with, where he
might go if he took off on purpose, and why he'd
go. If you know *where* he is, don't tell me; I need to
earn a fat fee right now."

Pederson looked at me and sighed. "This isn't a
clearinghouse of public information, it's a police
department. You," he tapped my side of the desk,
"aren't a cop. And I don't see why we'd know what
you want to find out. We're just as anxious to know
what happened to him as your client is, but there is
'insufficient evidence of foul play'—" he mimicked
a grand-jury pronouncement "—to call for a search
for Grey himself. You know that. We don't have
much official information, and what we do have we
don't pass out like Kleenex." For a cop, he looked
almost apologetic.

I shifted in my chair for the twentieth time. It
wasn't comfortable; it wasn't supposed to be, on
this side of the desk. "In that case, let's just talk.
Nothing official. I've come for a social call, and the
topic has just happened to turn to Stiff the Snow
Man. I wonder if you've heard anything about

where he went and what he was doing? Pure hear-say, of course."

He thought about it. He didn't like it, but he wanted to like it a lot. "About time you paid a social call anywhere. All right; understand, this is pure gossip—nothing to do with official business."

He went to a file cabinet against the wall and pulled out a thick, dog-eared yellow folder full of printouts. He looked them over, pulled out the most recent sheaf—the part that had handwriting on it—and asked innocently, "You don't mind a little malicious gossip, do you?"

"I used to hang around the bathrooms at high-school dances for it. Why do you keep a file of printouts when you could run off a new set anytime?"

Pederson walked over to the terminal and punched a code number. "Running them off like that is a waste of paper." The printer began chattering. "Besides, all those copies are hard to keep track of. If one disappeared, I wouldn't know where it had gone and neither would the department."

"That'd be a shame. I couldn't help noticing the scribbling on one of those printouts. Why isn't that information fed straight into the computer?"

He scowled at me. "Lazy typist." I knew he was supposed to type new data in himself. Jon hates computer terminals; he came to them too late in life.

He offered me coffee. I refused, saying coffee was expensive and I was a taxpayer, goddammit, and he poured me a cup anyway. It was awful coffee—bitter and black, the kind that reminds me I'm a tea drinker. I sipped at it and he worked while we waited for the machine to finish.

Finally it stopped. He sighed, got up slowly and moved across the room, looking old and tired. He tore the last sheet off and brought the pile of papers back to his desk. "We were talking about Stiff the Snow Man." He glanced at the handwritten notes on the old printout. "Say, I heard something strange the other day—"

"Excuse me," I said with my best straight face. "You have any scratch paper? I like to doodle while I listen." He nodded absently and pointed to the pile of papers he had just run off. I took it and thanked him; the desk didn't look appreciably neater.

We could have gone on kidding ourselves like that for a half hour. Instead, I got my pencil and Pederson dictated new "hearsay" in an offhand voice. It wasn't hard to tell the written parts from the ad-libs.

"Since you ask, Mr. Phillips, I do remember something or other I heard about Steven Grey. He was, you remember, acquitted when he was tried for the murder of Ed Grogan over two years ago. Somehow nobody saw anything; the D.A. couldn't do more than make the jury suspicious of Grey, and nobody gets sent up on that little. Since then, even before then, really, Grey has never done anything illegal, to our knowledge." Pederson looked at me quickly. I tried to look interested and nothing more.

He started reading again. "Of course, that doesn't mean people haven't been suspicious, but nothing has ever been proven. His import business has always looked legitimate—"

"You mean he's occasionally imported something, just to confuse people," I said. Pederson took no notice.

"But in the past two-and-a-half years, he has had a partner, one with an . . . unusual business record."

I looked up at him this time. He paused and said, "Interested?"

"Maybe I'd better hear some more, uh, gossip. What about this business partner?"

Pederson smirked. "One of those things the D.A.'s office didn't bother to tell you and Cartley while you worked for them. This is the kind of gossip I love. Benny Rosetti came to work for Steve Grey just before the trial—about the time all the witnesses rushed out to have their eyes checked, their brains laundered and their memories shortened. You see, Rosetti used to work in New York. He left town for business reasons, right after an organized-crime killing.

"He used to work in Chicago. He left town for business reasons, right after an organized-crime killing. He used to work in Los Angeles, Denver, San Francisco, Cincinnati and Miami; he left each of them for business reasons, right after an organized—"

"Are you telling me something or reciting poetry?" I said. "I get the point. What's Rosetti's official job?"

Pederson peered at the handwritten comments dubiously. "He seems to be some sort of free-lance executive."

"How coy. Did anyone ever try to pin down what exactly it is he executes?"

"Only courts in Cincinnati, Chicago and all points west. Strangely, New York, Newark and Miami never did a thing; tell me I'm surprised. No convictions in any of the cases—not because of scared witnesses, either; there just plain weren't any. Insufficient evidence every time."

"Was there any resemblance between the murders—anything pointing to the same man in each case?"

"You're not going to like this—especially if your work sends you to Rosetti."

I shrugged, overdoing it. "Go on. To hell with the blindfold."

He sighed. "All right, Superman, be that way. Besides the lack of witnesses, everything else about the murders was identical but the city and the victim. They were all done outdoors. They were all done with a .22 pistol. The victims were all untouched, except for the bullet holes—oh, yes, they all had two bullet holes, almost exactly an inch above the heart, one or the other of them through the aorta. No powder burns."

I sat very still, and the hair on the back of my neck crawled up and down as if it were unhappy and wanted to hide somewhere. "No powder burns?"

"None. All the ballistics experts agreed the shots were fired from at least six feet away. Not one shot was more than thirty-one or less than twenty-four millimeters above a line across the top of the heart—as neatly done as if they were contact wounds. The killer's aim couldn't have been better if he'd used a target rifle and a tripod, instead of a handgun."

"Why above the heart?"

I didn't sound calm enough; Pederson smiled. "The heart hops around a lot, and heart walls can be thick," he said softly. "A .22 slug is small—remember, that's hundredths of an inch, not millimeters—and if you shoot at the heart there's a chance that the bullets will lodge in the wall, instead of hitting a chamber. The aorta, though, carries an awful lot of blood and hardly jumps around at all. If you could put two shots right over a man's heart, you'd be certain to sever the aorta with one of them—if you knew where to shoot." He looked down at his folder and added, "Somebody does."

"Neat." I gave up on the back of my neck and

changed the subject. "What else does he do for fun?"

"Apparently, quite a bit. Several busts for cocaine; he's been a user for ten years. That doesn't help his other problem." He waited. I waited. He gave up and went on. "Benny Rosetti kills people for business. He beats them for pleasure. If you'll look at the last page of your, um, scratch paper, you'll see a mention of Rosetti's five arrests for assault."

"Beatings with coke or without?"

"All of them with, and all of them pretty brutal. I've seen the full reports, with photos, on two of the beatings: broken noses, broken jaws, missing teeth, severe concussions and internal bleeding—Rosetti was as sloppy about his personal fights as he is businesslike about his killings."

"Why did you say 'was'?" I asked.

I was supposed to ask. He threw me a smile. " 'Was' because, as far as anyone knows, he quit. The last complaint on him was three years ago. If he'd followed his own pattern, he'd have been arrested one or two years ago, everyone would have refused to testify against him, and he would have been released. Then he would have kept in control of himself for another year or so. From the looks of things, I'd say he's in control permanently now."

"A heartwarming story. How a poor but honest assassin, crippled by addiction, rose above his handicap to become—"

Pederson was shaking his head. "Cocaine's not addictive."

"Of course it is."

"No, it isn't."

"The hell you say."

"Can we stop sounding like junior high, Phillips? Cocaine users are psychologically dependent, that's all." He scowled. "That's what they tell me."

"Who says?"

"Doctors."

"Oh. Doctors. So cocaine addicts are only dependent, then." I thought. "Isn't that rough enough?"

"Seems it to me. Anyway, I never said Rosetti
quit using cocaine."

"But still he quit being abusive? Are you serious?
Coke users are notoriously self-indulgent; you
know that."

"Maybe so, but he hasn't left a bloodstained trail
of screaming victims and gory handprints. Plus, his
professional work these days—we've heard of a
couple of out-of-town jobs with his M.O.—hasn't
gotten any messier."

"That's all I need to know about him." More than
I wanted to, in fact. "You think he killed Grey?"

"If anyone did, he'd be the one. Just the same,
the police keep a pretty close eye on him, and he'd
find it hard to dispose of a body."

"I don't suppose his business competitors would
give him much peace, either. Who are the last
people who saw Grey alive?"

"That's information the police wouldn't—"

"Oh, come off it. You probably know the last time
Grey brushed his teeth after lunch. You may not be
investigating him or his associates, but you're sure
as hell not ignoring them."

Pederson answered, hurt, "I was going to go on; I
have some reliable gossip about the last people he
went to talk with."

"Oh. Sorry."

He glowered at me. "And they won't be much
help." He sounded glad. "Grey visited one of his
college professors, talked to a short-order cook he'd
been at school with and kept an appointment with a
business competitor named Reedy Rentschler.
Which one do you think he told his life story to?"

I grunted. He gave me addresses and skimmed the printout one last time, his lips moving rapidly.

He stopped, rereading something. "Oh—this really is gossip: about six months ago the desk sergeant received a complaint from a Hennepin Avenue hooker. The usual gripe is rough treatment; the department never does anything unless the girl insists—it's bad business for us and her. This girl got through the address of the john she had a complaint against, then said, 'Forget it,' and hung up. The desk man wrote down her name and the address of the john, anyway. We like to check these things against our records." He made another dramatic pause.

I'd had it with drama. "So?"

"So the address was Grey's. Rosetti's lived there since Grey disappeared."

I leaned forward. Pederson smiled; I don't know why cops are so fond of surprising people. I asked, "What's her name?"

"Deirdre Ryan. She works the corner of Fifth and Hennepin. We don't have her present address; it would be easy enough to get, but she'd only change it."

I thought a moment. "Anybody follow up the complaint?"

Pederson looked annoyed. "Are you kidding? We have enough business these days; we don't need to drum it up." He looked down at his desk and began sorting papers again.

That was my cue. I stood up, folding the printouts inside my newspaper carefully, and thanked him for his time. As I turned to leave, he said, "Nate—"

I turned around, trying to look like a punk. "Yeah?"

It didn't bother him. "The police gave you the case, or at least helped you get it, because you needed it—that, and I thought you'd want to keep busy for a while. You always had Roy to fall back on—'' He stopped. "I could have put that better.'' I didn't say anything. "What I'm trying to say, Nate, is this: you've worked by yourself before, but this time you don't have a partner to call when you need him. I'm sorry about that, and I know you are, too.''

He fussed with a paper clip. "You don't need to play hero, Nate, and you can't play as rough as the people you'll be talking to while you look for Grey. Call if and when you get in trouble.''

I didn't have any good replies ready. "Sure.''

He added awkwardly, "We should keep in touch now. You doing anything this Sunday night? Want to have dinner with Willa and me?''

"Thanks, but I guess for a while I'll be busy.''

He nodded. "Out with those screwball friends of yours?''

"Not lately.'' Then I realized I'd misunderstood him. "Yeah, sure,'' I lied.

"What about that one that's always mixed up with women? What's-his-name—Bernie. He'll be there?''

"Probably.''

"You're pretty thick with him, aren't you? You see him all the time?'' Even when a cop's concerned for his friends, he gives them the third degree.

I shifted. "He was at the funeral, remember?''

"Oh, yes.'' Jon looked embarrassed.

"Other than that, I haven't seen much of him the past few days.'' I checked my watch. "Look, I've got to go.''

He knew damn well I didn't have anywhere to go. "See you.''

On my way through the door, I bumped into two patrolmen bringing a shabbily dressed man with a little mustache. He seemed distracted—he couldn't focus on anything very long. I thought he was an accident victim until he leaned forward and said conspiratorially, ''I shot my wife this afternoon. What did you do?''

I leaned toward him and asked in the same tone, ''You the guy from Summit Avenue?''

''Yeah,'' he said proudly, and didn't seem to notice he was starting to cry. ''What did you do?''

''Nothing, yet.'' I left the police station and went to my office. I had some printouts to read through before I started the legwork tomorrow.

3

THE NEXT MORNING I tucked the printouts under one arm and my cat Marlowe under the other and headed downstairs to the car. I set Marlowe down by the front door. He made a disapproving noise. I put him back inside, just to show who was boss. He made another disapproving noise. I let him back out and said, "You're a pleasure to work for. I better not have this much fuss around the door when I get back." He made a final noise and slunk down the front step.

I got in my car and drove to Chesterfield College; I wanted to see the professor Grey had been talking with before Grey disappeared. The school was in Cold Plains, only forty miles south of the Twin Cities; it was a pleasant quick drive. The frost on the bridges and overpasses was already gone in the spring sunlight.

Chesterfield was on a hill on the east side of town. The buildings were mostly either gray-concrete simulated Gothic or red-brick imitation Norman; both types dated from around nineteen hundred. I drove slowly and savored the aura of synthetic history. The campus was open, well planned and covered with oaks, maples and cedars. You just knew that in spring and fall there was ivy growing all over the school. You also knew that the college watered it carefully all through the hot months; midwestern colleges are self-conscious about their ivy.

The administrative offices would be unhappy about my presence; instead of getting directions from them I asked a pretty red-haired girl in a green army parka. She smiled and showed me which building housed the English department. I had to park my car and walk; in the late sixties the campus had closed to all traffic. Back then it must have seemed absurd; now all the colleges were doing it. Nobody yells about the rights of drivers with the cost of gas as high as it is.

At the English department they had a directory posted. I found the listing I wanted: Professor Michael Davies, room 204. I went up the broad, curving lobby stairs. The English department, like everything else on campus, was in a building designed to look older than it really was; I got the feeling Chesterfield College was very big on very young traditions.

The office wasn't as large or as obvious as I'd expected—I missed it twice. The door was open; two people were talking inside. I heard a querulous mumble from a youngster, then heard a rich humor-filled voice say, "Come now, Mr. Pedretti—can you really expect me to enthuse over a two-page attempt at a comprehensive elucidation of the afterlife? That's like asking me to enthuse over a two-page version of *War and Peace*."

The kid was silent. I tried to think of anything he could say back and decided that if he were smart, he'd grovel right out the door.

He was smart. He bumped into me in the doorway as he slunk out, putting on his coat and muttering to himself. "Relax," I said as he apologized. "By the time you're a sophomore you'll be writing papers that have him begging for more."

He glared at me. "I'm a junior now."

"Oh. Sorry. Well, good luck next year, but

remember, there's no pleasing some people." He shrugged and went on his way. I knocked on the door frame.

"Come in." The voice was commanding, like a victorious general's.

The office was smaller on the inside. They all are, but this one was smaller by a good two feet. Three of the walls were lined with bookshelves. The shelves were jammed with old books, battered books, a few tattered paperbacks and an occasional shiny new book with a glossy dust jacket. The fourth wall had a window, two great stacks of filing cabinets and a desk.

Seated at the desk, smoking one of the vilest cigars I've ever run across, was a man in his mid-fifties. He was stocky but not overweight, balding, with a residue of fine red hair. He had a firm jaw that made me think of road-crew foremen and straw bosses more than it did of English professors. In his left hand was a journal; in his right was a pen, poised over an index card.

He looked up and realized I wasn't a student. "What can I do for you, sir?" he said around the cigar.

"I'm not in a hurry. If you want, you can fill out the card first."

He nodded, put his cigar in an ashtray—I expected the ashtray to choke—and began scribbling rapidly, talking to me as he did. "I can see you're a long way from being a student; seldom is such patience displayed in my office. This will only take a minute. I'm annotating an article to take the taste of bad prose out of my mouth."

"Is it working?"

"Not terribly well; it just reminds me not to be too hard on college students for making fools of themselves in the manner of full-fledged professors." He

finished the card with a flourish and put it on a pile
of similar cards. "I'll type these up tomorrow morning, when it's too early for me to think. And now,
sir, may I help you?"

He looked like a man I'd better not lie to. "Yes,
but not with literature just now." I showed him a
photostat of my license. He examined it closely and
handed it back.

"You're what the thrillers of my early youth
called a shamus," he said, poker-faced. "I trust
you're not after any of my present students. I
rather hope I've been reading and correcting their
biggest crimes to date."

His diction was catching. "I'm trying to locate a
former student of yours. He's been missing for some
time, and my client fears something is amiss."

He raised an eyebrow, put his cigar back in his
mouth and thought for a moment, frowning. "I
assume it would be violating your professional
ethics for me to ask the name of your client?"

"Only if I told you."

"I see." He seemed nettled. "Since the police
have already inquired after him once, since they
asked when he was expected back, and since he
hasn't visited recently, I assume you're looking for
Steven Grey." He motioned me to a chair.

I sat down. "You're right. If you don't mind my
saying so, you wouldn't do badly in my line of
work."

He nodded, pleased. "Scholars are detectives already—if they're good scholars." He hesitated,
then said, "But I won't waste your time and mind
with brilliant near-miss guesses at the obvious. I'm
sure your time is as valuable as mine."

"Oh, I don't know. You work with budding pro-
fessionals and academics; I work with criminals."

He grimaced. "Your presence shows that the two

categories aren't as distinct as I'd like to believe."

I leaned forward. "That brings me to the first question. Why would Steven Grey visit you? No offense intended, of course, but you don't seem like the criminal type any more than he did the be-true-to-your-school type."

Professor Davies shifted and stubbed out his cigar. I wanted to thank him. "I'll answer that, Mr. Phillips, if you'll tell me what importance you attach to the answer."

I studied my nails for a moment, building my patience and thinking. He had a right to ask. I wasn't the police, and he didn't know me or my client. "I know very little about Grey," I admitted finally, "including whether or not he's still alive." The professor looked surprised and upset at the suggestion. "I'll stand a better chance of finding him if I know a little about him. There might be other people he would visit for the same reasons he came to you."

Davies sighed. "So someone else believes in motivations. I thought no one did but outdated literary critics."

"Call me a sentimental old fool, but I still believe people do things for reasons."

He responded dryly, "So do I. If you don't mind my saying so, you wouldn't do badly in my line of work."

"Not a chance—I move my lips when I read."

"Some people would call that lecturing." He sat back in his swivel chair. "I'll answer your question, but you won't like the answer. He visited me for two reasons: because he knew and liked me, and because I made him feel guilty."

"I'm not sure whether I like it or not; I don't understand."

Davies lit up a cigar again. "I don't, either—but some people are like that; they'd rather be around

people that make them miserable, punishing themselves. Steven took a course in Morality in Literature from me; sometimes I think he confused me
with a judge.''

"Don't worry; he got straightened out on that."

Davies frowned. "You're sure? At any rate, he'd
come down to visit at least twice a term—just drop in
my office unannounced and talk. Sometimes he'd
bring up literature, sometimes he'd ask about the
college, sometimes he'd ask after my family. Always
he would bring up the topics, and always before they
were done he'd blush and say very little.''

I tried imagining Stiff the Snow Man, suspected of
murder and of running the largest drug ring in the
Twin Cities, blushing in this office. I had a hard
time.

"Then we'd just talk about little details—the
kinds of things two people talk about when they
don't have as much to say as they want to have.''

"I didn't imagine he'd talk shop. Was anything
different about his last visit?"

"It was just after his trial. The first thing I did was
congratulate him on being acquitted.''

I looked surprised. Davies noticed and said gruff-
ly, "I was glad he was acquitted, and I still am." He
looked out his window, brooding. "Morally, perhaps, I'm not so happy, but I can't help being glad
when one of my students has escaped a life sentence.''

"I don't suppose it made you happy to realize you
were probably congratulating a killer.''

He stubbed his cigar out a second time. "The law
says he was not a murderer, and I trust the law."
He added grudgingly, "Principally because I want
to in this case.''

It wasn't my business, so I let it drop. "What did
he say when you congratulated him?"

He didn't answer right away. There was a lot to hink about, apparently. "First," he said slowly, 'he flushed and wouldn't look at me. Then, when ie saw that I really was happy for him, he smiled. I lon't think too many people were glad for him; he ilways seemed pretty lonely."

Maybe it was his voice, or a trick with words or ny own situation just then, but suddenly I could see irey as Davies did and sympathize. I could under-tand why Grey would keep visiting Davies, too; I'd iad an older friend myself, in my partner. They can ie special. "What happened then?"

"Then he told me—" He stopped. His eyes looked iurt.

I waited. He didn't say anything. "He told you—" prompted.

"That doesn't mean I'll tell you."

I realized I was rushing him. "Look, Professor)avies, I can't tell you who my client is, but I can ell you that it's someone who wants to find him 'ery badly: not to arrest him—I'm not a cop—but to :now whether he's alive or dead."

He regarded me skeptically. "Steven Grey didn't hink there was one person on earth worried about iim for any reason but profit."

"I'm not so sure my client isn't interested for)rofit, but I might as well give the benefit of the loubt."

"To whom?"

"To everyone involved; we'll all need it."

He almost smiled. "Then I'll tell you—not out of iny confidence in your client's motives, but be-:ause I'm giving *you* the benefit of the doubt. After congratulated him, he told me that his mother :alled him at the jail while the jury was out, ind he was allowed to take the call." He stopped igain.

He needed prodding. I said, "You don't need to stop for me. I'm not taking notes just now."

He said coldly, "She wanted him to know she had offered her services to the prosecution as a character witness—I should say, as a defamation-of-character witness. The District Attorney turned her down; aside from the complications of having a relative testify, he felt—probably rightly—that it would only make the defendant look pathetic."

I gritted my teeth. I don't like working for liars. I hadn't liked Mrs. Grey to start with, and I was pretty sure I never would. Professor Davies was grinning. "Aha. Touch a nerve?"

Private detective, hell. He would have made a good cop. I answered, hoping it was convincing, "I helped the D.A.'s office look for witnesses on that case. Nobody told me a thing about his mother." Including his mother.

He nodded. "I hesitate to say it, but perhaps our District Attorney is an honorable man. It pleases me to think so."

"You and Diogenes. Now, if you don't mind my asking, did he say anything about planning a trip anywhere?"

He replied immediately, "No. The police asked that, you know." Pretty thorough for not having investigated. "About the only thing he said was the usual twaddle about trying to get back in control of his life." Davies looked annoyed, then suddenly intrigued. "No. Come to think of it, he said his life *and* his business." He looked at me. "Redundant, of course."

"Of course." I wondered how Grey thought he could get back in control of his business once he'd let Rosetti in. "Did he at least say what he was planning to do?"

"I don't think he knew. He acted like he wasn't happy and wasn't likely to be."

"How romantic. You make him sound more like a poet than a criminal."

Davies looked pleased. "You know, he once wanted to be a poet. Steven always was very fond of poetry. As a matter of fact," he said, rummaging around in his desk, "he brought me a line or three the last time he was here. Do you want to see them?"

I nodded, not really caring. The only thing I'd learned here so far was how to dislike Elizabeth Grey more thoroughly.

He shuffled through more papers, muttering to himself about straightening. As far as I could tell, the only thing out of place was the scrap he was looking for. Finally he pounced on a folder, drew it out and handed a scrap from it to me. It was only three lines:

For the listener, who listens in the snow,
And, nothing himself, beholds
Nothing that is not there and the nothing that is.

I handed it back. "Strange. Is it his or somebody else's?"

He looked at me curiously. "If you don't mind the quiz, I'd like to see what a detective makes of it. What do you think?"

I was annoyed, but scratched the top of my head and thought. "Well, I'd say it's a quote from a longer poem, from the way the first line sort of dangles. If that's right, then I'd say it's somebody else's. Writers usually send the whole of any work they do themselves; they can't bear to chop it into little pieces."

He clapped silently. "Bravo. It is the last stanza of a poem by Wallace Stevens, a poem called 'The Snow Man.'"

"Thank you. Would you mind just telling me things like that?"

"My apologies. For a living I teach people to think; it gets habit forming. There are two questions about this poem that I can't answer, however: why did he give it to me, and what does it mean?"

I looked at the scrap. "Mmm. Well, I can see why he chose this poem, now that you've told me the title." He looked blank. "Professor, stop thinking of snow as white stuff you shovel; Grey was a cocaine and morphine dealer, among other things. You say he felt guilty. Maybe he felt worthless, felt like the nothing that isn't there and the nothing that is; the lines may mean something else in context, but quoted by him they sound like guilt, shame and a little sorrow at his own worthlessness." Davies grunted. "And since he gave it to you, I suppose he meant you as the listener. Does that make sense?"

He thought a moment, then shook his head violently. "It does, except for something you don't have here. The first line of the poem is 'One must have a mind of winter'; 'one' refers, I've always assumed, to 'the listener.' I've never acted coldly toward Grey; sometimes I've been almost the only one who didn't."

"I'm afraid that only makes my case stronger," I said gently. "The line doesn't say one has it, it says one *must* have it. From that, and from what you say about his attitude, it sounds like he knew he was going to try something risky, maybe something that could be fatal. He gave you this, since you were—probably—the only person who'd be upset if anything happened to him; he wanted to brace you for it without coming out and saying so."

He looked at me for a moment, looked blankly and unhappily, like a man being told of a friend's death. He stared out the window and said nothing. After a moment he opened the window.

"I hope you don't mind." He lit the stub of his cigar. "It's warm out, and I like the smell of fresh air."

"How can you tell?" I stared pointedly at his cigar.

He grinned and blew a cloud of noxious smoke out the window. "Well, sir, do you have any more questions?"

"Just one. Do you know of anyone else Grey would have gone to when he felt bad or was in trouble? Are there any other people he talked about often, about going to or talking to?"

He pulled at his lower lip thoughtfully, putting the cigar in his left hand and dangling it over the ashtray while he thought. Presently a half inch of powdery ash fell off the cigar into the ashtray. Neat trick.

"Harry Fogerty. He runs a diner in Saint Paul. Harry and Steven weren't close in school but they got to be much better friends after graduation. You can get the address out of the Saint Paul phone book: Harry's Fine Diner." He glanced meaningfully at the notebook in my shirt pocket.

I wrote down the name and the diner, even though I had them both already. I thanked him, then left behind one of my cards and asked him to get in touch if he heard from Grey. "It's been nice talking to you. Now I go back to footwork."

He looked as pained as I had. "And I go back to paperwork," he said, and grimaced. He picked up a sheaf of papers and held them out to me hopefully.

"You wouldn't be interested in correcting twenty freshman essays, thirteen of which are on abortion, drugs or capital punishment, would you?"

"You wouldn't be interested in talking to a few cocaine addicts, a gunman and drug dealer, and a Hennepin Avenue streetwalker, would you?"

He considered. "I guess I'll stick with the papers." He put them down and shook hands with me. "It was close, though."

4

ON MY WAY OUT I stopped at the registrar's office, but they wouldn't tell me anything. Grey had the right-to-privacy regulations protecting his records—not even he could get any information about himself without being there in person; a phone call wouldn't do it. As for me, the registrar wouldn't have told me whether it had snowed while Grey was at school.

I gave up, went to a truck stop for lunch and made it back to Minneapolis by two o'clock. I drove on up to my office to finish out the day, following Professor Davies's example: filing, straightening and feeling intellectually virtuous.

When the knock came on my door I was reading the papers stuffed in the back of a file, wondering who Louie Shapiro had been and if his file was worth storing or not if I couldn't remember. My desk was an inch deep in mislabeled file folders, both Roy's and mine. I said, "Come in." Somehow my voice didn't have Davies's authoritative ring.

My visitor didn't rate a snappier delivery. He walked in, looked around once and sneered at me. "Cheap and easy, cheap and easy," he cackled.

"Pleased to meet you, Mr. Easy. I'm Nate. Now that we know each other, you want to say what you're here for? I don't clean clothes," I added.

He didn't take offense. How could he? God knows he must have been told and called worse often

enough. His pants had grease, dirt, mud and three
or four colors of unidentifiable but revolting stains
on them. His shirt and jacket had once been red
flannel and brown-and-white check, respectively;
now they nearly matched. His boots looked like several dogs had fought with them and lost. I couldn't
see his socks. I was grateful.

He didn't look much better than his clothes. He
was five foot ten or so, and weighed maybe a hundred pounds in muggy weather. His eyes were red
rimmed and small pupiled; the whites were shellac
yellow. His arms were skinny, his fingers wiry. If
he'd had better bones he might have looked like a
skeleton; as it was, he looked made of Tinkertoys
and beat-up ones at that. His wrists had prominent,
unhealthy-looking veins; you didn't have to look at
them twice to know his arms were covered with
tracks farther up. He looked an aging sixty but was
probably a decrepit forty-five.

His nose was red and flaking; it must have dried
up early and often. Most of his skin that showed
had scratch marks; he'd been doing coke long
enough to have a D.T.'s-style itch. His mouth was
the most disturbing thing about him; it was a cross
between a cokie's detached, superior smile and a
good ol' boy's sloppy grin. Dirty, decaying men with
vicious habits shouldn't look so agreeable.

"Now," I said, "tell me what you want here, but I
bet I don't sell it."

He leered at me. "Don't talk to me like that. I
could break you in half, little man."

I gaped. "No, you couldn't," I said simply. "I
mean, I don't want to hurt your feelings, but you
don't look like you could break a promise without
help."

His shoulders sagged. He said dejectedly, "I was
just trying to talk gangster talk."

I was touched. "You did a good job; I was just trying to talk tough back at you."

"You?" He grinned and patted my arm. I wanted to wash it. "Why, you don't even have any chest hair."

"I wear sweaters a lot. What are you here for?"

He leaned forward and stared into my face in an effort to frighten me. I was terrified; I just knew he hadn't brushed his teeth in weeks. "Lay off trying to find Stiff the Snow Man, or you'll be in big trouble. There are people that don't want you to go on looking—got it?" He stepped back. I exhaled, wondering how "people" knew about my new case.

"What are they going to do to me if I keep on?"

He grinned self-consciously. "Heck, I don't know. They just told me to tell you that."

"Why'd they pick you to tell me?"

"Oh, I don't know," he said, biting at a fingernail. "They just wanted to send a message cheap, I guess. These guys, see, they gave me a skinful for later and a fin for now, and they told me what to say."

"If they wanted to be cheap they could have sent a postcard. Who were these guys, anyway?"

He got a crafty look in his eyes and said, "Oh, no, I won't tell. They said they had more work for me this afternoon if I did this right, and I can sure use the money." Then he looked solemn and added, "I'll tell you this, though: they really are tough." He nodded ten or fifteen times to show how much he thought they were tough. "When they throw their weight around, I bet things break."

"Bubbles, potato chips, hearts?" I was tired, I'd driven a long way, and I don't like being threatened even on good days.

He looked at me disgustedly. "You can say that now easy enough, young fella, but see how you feel when they talk to you with their fists."

"That's what I still don't get. If they wanted to scare me, why not send a tough?"

He chewed on that for a while, then had an idea. "Maybe they don't want you to know what they look like, so it's easier to jump you."

That didn't sound funny. I thought about it for all of twenty seconds. "Nah. They wouldn't have bothered sending you at all, then. If you're going to jump someone, you don't send out invitations."

He shrugged. "Doesn't matter. You got your warning, I got my pay, and we're both happy."

"Who said I was happy?"

He said, as if it made all the sense in the world, "But I didn't come to make you happy; couldn't you just be satisfied?"

"Okay, fine, I'm satisfied. I've got to go back to work. Thanks for coming." I started sorting papers again. When I looked up a minute later he was still there. I gave him my best glassy stare. "Well?"

He produced his sloppy grin again and held out his hand for money. "Any reply?"

Who could be mad at a panhandler that brassy? I handed him two dollars. "Yeah. 'Have a happy day. love, Mom.'"

He looked at his palm disdainfully. "That isn't much money."

"It isn't much of a message. Next time I'll just write a note. Now go deliver it."

He left. I thought about sweeping the floor where he'd been standing. It could wait. I went back to wondering who Louie Shapiro was and why Roy's files had to be such a mess.

At five I locked up the files, cleaned off my desk top, pulled on my stocking cap and left. The drive home was good, but in spite of the forecast it was starting to get chilly. Behind me I could see clouds piling up—ugly gray ones that made the sunset look even prettier and the growing darkness even grimmer. Tonight and tomorrow night not be pleasant.

I parked my car across from my apartment. When I turned to get out I saw that someone was leaning on my stairway door. I pulled my .38 from the shoulder holster as I got out of the car, slipping the gun in my pocket as I slammed the door. I walked over—not too quickly, not too casually.

It was the message man from that afternoon. His face was badly scraped up, and his lower lip was split and swollen. He was leaning on the door for support, breathing in short, pained gasps. He was holding his left arm awkwardly, trying to cradle it against his body. Great fat tears were rolling down his cheeks.

As I ran up to him he fell against me. I caught him in my left arm and had my gun out and my back to the door as fast as I could spin. Nobody moved. A newspaper blew past in the street. I listened. All I could hear were a record player next door wailing about broken hearts and a faint hum from the freeway a block and a half away.

I shifted so he could lean more comfortably and started walking him to the car. "Why did they do it?" I asked.

"I don't know. I don't know," he whimpered, stumbling, and nearly toppled us both. "I came back and asked what the second message was, and they started in on me. First they slugged my gut, then roughed up my face, then one of them held my arm and the other took a tire iron and—" He started to cry.

I patted his shoulder carefully and opened the car door for him. "It won't be long. I'll get you to a hospital." As he got in he had to let go of his arm; it dangled for a second, bending oddly, and he screamed. He dove in, falling on his back on the seat, clutching his arm and rocking to and fro.

I ran around to the other side. Before I got in I took one last quick look around. Nobody, not a soul; the whole neighborhood might have been hiding in basements, holding its breath. By now it was totally dark.

I turned the car around and headed north for Abbott Hospital. My passenger groaned every time we hit a bump. "Brace up. We'll be there soon. How many times did they hit you on the arm?"

"Twice." He sat up, slowly and carefully. As we passed the Institute of Arts he said, puzzled and pained, "But they said I could deliver the second message. They never told me what it was, though."

New ideas sink in slowly, but I was beginning to understand. "How did you get to my doorway?"

"They drove there and threw me out," he said listlessly. "What of it?"

"Then that's why they picked you for the first message," I said. "You *were* the second message." I pulled into the Emergency driveway.

5

FROM THE HOSPITAL I told the police what had happened and to whom. All I could tell them was his name—Joey Heinicke. All they could tell me was that his nickname was Greasy Joe, which didn't surprise me, and that he was a petty thief and a coke-hound that nobody much cared about. They seemed unhappy that somebody had bothered to break his arm.

Well, so was I. It seemed like a lot of trouble for a simple threat. I stayed around till the doctor saw to him, then took off. He could take care of himself; it wasn't like I was his mother.

Joe hadn't told me much in the waiting room; the men who beat him sounded like straight toughs, cheap thugs. Only one thing disturbed me: they had known what he wanted, where to find him and how much to offer him. That meant they knew his supplier. Whoever planned this threat did his homework.

Well, two things: they also had known the minute I got the case.

I quit thinking about it. I was too restless to go home just yet; I went to Saint Paul over the Franklin Avenue Bridge. It took a while that way, but it kept me off the freeway; since Roy's death I was still a little spooked about driving. It got me to downtown Saint Paul just the same.

Downtown Saint Paul has been going downhill

long enough to be America's deepest valley. On my way through it I passed four adult bookstores and movie theaters, two rubber-novelty shops and an all-night liquor store with rows of thick sweet wines for two bucks a gallon. Pawnshops, secondhand bookstores, dead businesses run by sickly businessmen.

It was like that in the thirties, when Ma Barker and her family of bank robbers hid out and the city government knew they were there. It was like that in the late fifties and early sixties when everywhere else the cities were screaming for urban renewal. To give it credit, it only got a little worse in the late seventies, when everything else was going downhill. Good times or bad, it didn't matter. Tough guys come, tough guys go, but downtown Saint Paul never changes. It's like dirty laundry—always around, always unsightly.

Harry's Fine Diner was a cut above the places around it. It was in a three-storey red-brick apartment building with a ground-floor storefront and upstairs apartments. The apartments had dirty white curtains instead of the usual torn window shades. In this neighborhood, that meant class.

Inside the diner—the part Harry could do something about—it was nice. There were shiny pink linoleum counter tops, and pink tabletops, and pink bar stools and benches. The stripe around the counter was pink. The water glasses and ashtrays were tinted pink, and the ceiling light gave off a soft pink glow. I looked at the place and wondered what Harry's favorite color was.

The menu was clean and the floors were clean. The customers weren't. I ignored them and sat at the counter. When Harry came over I ordered a hamburger and a cup of tea, adding that I wanted to talk.

He told me he was busy but he'd try to talk later. He was a tall, slow-looking guy, balding, with a little mustache and gold wire rims. He didn't smile much, but he didn't look unhappy, either.

He turned his back and started making sandwiches. I watched him; he only looked slow because he didn't hurry. His big deft hands shuffled the meat and cheese together and threw them on bread, then dealt them on plates, and he carried them around himself. A woman followed behind him, pouring coffee for tough dirty men who looked like they needed it.

The phone rang and rang. And rang—six times. Harry and the waitress stopped to listen to it. He said flatly to everyone, "Don't nobody answer it. It's my wife."

It rang four more times. The waitress glared at Harry, walked over and picked it up.

"Hello?" she asked dully, then turned to Harry and said in the same voice, "It's your wife."

"It's your wife," Harry mock-whispered in the waitress's voice. A few customers snickered as he glared back at her and snatched the phone. "Hello. Yes. Sure. No, I won't forget. Yes, I'll bring them. Sure, I will. Wouldn't dream of it." He looked around as if afraid of getting caught. None of the customers appeared to be listening closely. He lowered his voice. Close as I was, I could barely hear his next words. "Thanks for calling, honey. I'll see you when I get home, soon as I can."

He hung up, then snarled loudly, "Never satisfied. There's always something wrong."

Several of the regulars paid up then and left. The show was over. Harry called them by name as they went out. "See you, Jack. Hey, Willie, stay out of trouble. Larry, keep Willie out of jail long enough to get him back here tomorrow, will you?" They joked back and walked out. There were only a few people left, mostly derelicts having coffee and ham sandwiches—probably the closest they ever came to nutrition.

I ignored them; so did Harry. He walked over and said, "What did you want to talk about?"

"First I want to compliment you on the little skit you just put on."

He looked at me blankly, then suspiciously. He opened his mouth, but I cut him off. "Don't worry. I won't tell anybody. If I hadn't caught the last line I wouldn't have known a thing. She calls up like that every night?" I tried to sound friendly, sympathetic and tickled to death.

It worked. He grinned shamefacedly. "Yep. She calls every night I'm open. I asked her to; it gives the regulars something to come in for, a good laugh." He shrugged, not too convincingly. "Besides, I like to talk to her."

I said admiringly, "Sounds like you two have fun." I oozed empathy. "But why the hard-luck version? Why not do a romance over the phone, instead?"

He looked thoughtful. "The guys here are mostly downers, hard-luck stories themselves," he said slowly. "They wouldn't get much of a kick out of a happy home or a telephone romance. It'd hurt them more than it'd please them. For most of them a wife that calls all the time is hard enough to imagine; a wife that calls because she loves you is painfully impossible." He wiped off a spot on the menu he'd just got back. "So, my wife calls—and I'm happy. She pretends to nag me—and they're happy." He looked at me and frowned.

"You don't look happy," I said brightly.

He was still frowning. "You said you wanted to talk to me. About what, and why?"

I showed him my photostated license, asked very quietly about Steven Grey and told him someone was concerned for Grey's welfare. He looked cynical.

"There are a lot more people concerned for his ill-fare." He turned and flipped three burgers on the grill as fast as I could flip playing cards. "But, anyway, it doesn't matter. What I can tell you couldn't help you kill him any more than it could help you find him." He threw three hamburger buns on the grill; the sizzle from meat and buns covered our conversation.

He leaned forward. "I know a little about his business," he muttered, "and I know him. He used to drop in here and talk."

"What about?"

"Oh, about college some—we were at the same school—but mostly about the times we knocked around together before I got married. We weren't good friends," he said hastily to my surprised look, "but I don't think he had any of those." He looked thoughtful again. "What he mostly had were bad friends in one form or another."

"I'm not interested in friends. In Grey's friends, I mean. What did Grey talk about?"

He drummed his fingers, annoyed. "We went to bars, plays and movies together once; we played a lot of pinball and tennis, and looked for girls. He talked about that. Don't rush me; I'm just talking for fun."

"Sorry. Remember, I'm just listening for business. He liked reminiscing with you, did he?"

"Not exactly." He put the burgers and buns together, threw them on a plate and yelled, "Doris!" The waitress came out, glared first at him and then at me, then took the burgers to a large man wearing a dirty T-shirt and sitting at the end of the bar. She glared at him, too. It didn't bother his appetite.

Harry turned back to me. "He didn't like coming in here. Remember I said something about derelicts being hurt by seeing happy homes? Steve was something like that. He knew how glad I was to get married and settle down and be in this business; it hurt him all the time. The difference between the derelicts and him is—" he lowered his voice still further "—Steven Grey kept coming back if he was hurt. I never knew anyone who spent more time setting himself up to be hurt. If you were hired by hoods to find Steve and shoot him, I'd be upset, but in a funny sort of way he would have hired you himself. He's a lost man, and if he ever finds himself, there'll be a death." He shook his head and began wiping the counter with a wet rag. "Sorry. I keep this place partly so I can think and spout off, and you're in the line of fire tonight."

"That's all right." I was thinking. I decided to risk it. "I heard somebody say he was a kind man."

"He was—to his friends."

"I heard somebody say he was kind to you."

Harry stopped wiping the counter. "He never was." His voice was cold, colder than the wind outside. "He wanted to be, but it just wasn't in his line of work. His idea of kindness was offering me a job."

"What kind of job?"

"His." He threw the rag down and began holding glasses to the light and polishing them, one by one. "He wanted me to work in his import business. All I did was keep account books of numbers, amounts of money and initials. He said the numbers were purchases by weight, legal ones. I should have known better; maybe I really did.

"I finally did for sure, about a month and a half after I'd started work. There was some kind of fuss in the front of his store. I heard some loud snaps like a board being dropped. The warehouse had concrete floors; I didn't think anything of it. I went back to accounting imports and wondering where the books on duty taxes were kept.

"All of a sudden Steve burst in, grabbed my arm and hustled me out the back. He said there was trouble between him and a customer, a jealous husband. Even then I didn't believe him. His left shoulder was bleeding, and he had a gun in his other hand. He said he was all right and told me to go home. I wanted to take him to a doctor, but he wouldn't go.

"That was in January, during a cold snap. That night he came pounding on my apartment door at two in the morning, cold and wet and wild eyed. He had a homemade bandage on his shoulder, and the pocket had been torn off his coat. He said he was freezing to death, would I let him in? I made him some coffee. He didn't say anything—just gulped it down, staring into space. When he finished it he thanked me and left.

"The next morning the papers said a big syndicate drug dealer named Dumont had been killed right at press time, thrown off the Washington Avenue Bridge near U. Minn. at about one in the morning. I guess you read about it—and about what the body had in its hand."

"They couldn't follow it up," I answered. "Finding one overcoat in the Twin Cities is like isolating one little old lady in Sun City, Arizona. The pocket is still at the Minneapolis police station—unless the County took it; river cases have jurisdiction problems. Anyway, the coat is probably long gone."

Harry said evasively, "I never saw Grey wear that coat again, and I never spoke about that evening. I quit my job the next morning—walked out and started looking for jobs. I'd saved up enough, so I bought this place."

"Why, how moral of you. And you never said anything about the coat to the police, and you just happen to mention it now?"

He didn't react. "I had no real evidence, and I didn't want to turn him in when I could be wrong," he said firmly. "And I didn't quit just to be moral; I left because I don't like that kind of work. I taught high school math once, and I quit that for the same reason. Two things to stay away from: criminals and adolescents."

"Come on; you were an adolescent once."

He said with satisfaction, "Everybody stayed away from me, too." He added, "As for telling you, what difference does it make? If he's all right, he'll have you killed; if he's dead, it can't hurt. Still want to find him?" It was a good day for threats.

I stirred my coffee. He turned and yelled to Doris, "Check the grill; it's getting greasy."

"Why me?" she said crossly.

He gestured at me. "Because I'm busy, and he won't."

"He didn't ask me nicely," I said. "Maybe if you did—"

"It'd be messier buttering up you than cleaning the grill." She picked up a spatula.

I asked Harry, "Did Grey feel guilty about his work, you think?"

"Sure. No question. He'd come in and ask how I was doing and if Sandy was okay, and how I liked the restaurant business, and then he'd say a little about his business—nothing much, just how much money he was making and not to worry about anything I read about him in the papers." He looked upset for a moment. "He always acted like he was guilty—every minute of his life."

"Who could blame him?"

Harry slammed his hand on the counter top.

"That's the strange part, though—he couldn't, himself. I think he felt guilty for what he did without shouldering the blame."

"That's a little complicated for me. Go on." I had a feeling where the story would lead.

"All right, let me give you an example. Once, back when we were in college, Steve had got involved with this girl who hung on him all the time—wouldn't do anything without him. Things got sour between them, and he worried about how to break it off. She was really neurotic about it, complete with crying jags and a hint about suicide attempts. We all knew about it; you can't keep things like that secret at a small school.

"A group of us were sitting around the lounge one day, and he walked in and said, 'Well, I've dropped her.' He tried to grin, but you could tell he was upset. Some idiot half joked that it was a rotten thing to do, and Grey turned and said, 'They don't break.' Just like that, he said it: 'They don't break when you drop them—not too many of them bounce, but they don't break.' He walked out and said over his shoulder, 'I learned that from my mother.' "

Harry scrubbed at a timeworn stain faded into the counter, then looked me in the eye. "I ask you, is that any kind of thing for a guy to pin on his mother?"

I poked at my dirty napkin. "Ever met her?"

"Who—his mother? No."

"You're right; it was rotten. But don't worry about her—if anybody ever tried to pin anything at all on her, she'd have an alibi." I put a quarter by my teacup and paid the tab.

As I left I turned in the doorway; Harry was the only person near it. I said, "Maybe he liked to talk to you because you and he were both misfits in your college class. Transplanted 'Ivy Leaguers' becoming a cocaine dealer and a short-order cook.''

He nodded. "That's part of it. There's probably a little friendship still from our business connection, too.''

I shook my head. "That's not a business that makes friendships. Partnerships and partners die young and fast. I think he may have admired you—quite a bit even—for cutting out of a bad business at a bad time financially.''

He thought about that while I left. He thought a lot and cleaned things a lot. They both seemed to do him good.

The way back through Saint Paul was just as dirty and just as decayed. I got home, fed Marlowe and apologized for being late—cats don't accept apologies, but they do expect them—and sat down to have a late dinner of leftovers and police printouts. I found the shoot-out at Grey's warehouse (no charges, nobody found), and there was a line or two trying to tie in Dumont's murder with Grey or his lieutenants. Grey's lieutenants themselves didn't seem to have much personality; they came, stumbled and went into jail with monotonous regularity.

I looked at the activities Grey was unprovably involved in—narcotics, prostitution, assault, perhaps two murders—and thought about the man everybody called "such a nice guy." Two murders. A nice guy.

Surprisingly, there was no evidence connecting Grey with blackmail. His mother must have been thinking of some other well-loved relative.

I made some tea and thought about him till late. Then I had a drink and went to bed, to dream of clean-cut boys in college sweaters. Some were flipping hamburgers; most of them were shooting at me and breaking people's arms.

6

THE NEXT DAY I went to the office early and went through my mail. One piece was a check, due these three months past; I greeted it as I would a lost lamb, then mailed a check for half its amount to Mrs. Cartley. There was a note from her, thanking me for being a pallbearer and saying would I visit when I had the time. And there was a copy of Roy's accident report, ordered more from sentiment than suspicion.

Since we had listed Roy's car as a business vehicle, the report was easy to get. It was dull reading; the other driver had confessed to being drunk and careless, and had plea bargained his way down to a light jail sentence. I was disgusted—not at the light sentence, but at the matter-of-fact stupidity of the accident report. Roy had been a good man who took plenty of risks for good causes, and in the end his death didn't mean a damn thing.

I tossed the report aside and endorsed the incoming check. While I was doing that, a head with dirty curls on it stuck itself around a corner, and Greasy Joe said between ample tooth gaps, "You busy?" He sniffled.

"Me? Never. Come in." Good thing I hadn't bothered to sweep up last night.

He swaggered in, one thumb hooked in his belt loops, the other arm in a plaster cast that already had a couple of dubious looking stains on it. His jacket was buttoned at the top and draped over the cast. I said, "For both our sakes, I hope you haven't got a message. How's the arm?"

He leaned over the desk. "Fine, fine." I drew back. He sniffed at me and blinked. Before I could reach for a Kleenex, he'd wiped his nose on a sleeve that was already stiff enough to stand away from the arm by itself. "But what I came in for is, I been investigating."

"What?" I was too startled to laugh.

"The guys that set me up." He sniffled again; this time I got him a Kleenex in time.

"You ought to take something for those sniffles, Joe."

He mumbled, "Later. I got business."

I was impressed. "You mean to tell me you aren't coking these days?"

"I didn't mean to tell you," he said truculently, "but I ain't using that stuff till I nail the guys that got me." He rubbed at his nose and wiped his eyes. "Let's not talk about it. It gets hard."

"I can imagine," I said slowly. "Why tell me you're going to get them?"

"Because," he replied sullenly, "you need help with your work, and I need it with mine. I sort of figured we could trade off and play partners until one or the other of us got finished. You're still trying to find Stiff Grey, aren't you?"

"What if I am?"

He snorted. "I knew it. I knew you didn't scare easy; you got plenty of guts, for a young fella. Now, what I figure is, you help me either get the two monkeys that beat me up or get their boss; maybe throw him and them in jail. I'll help dig up stuff on Grey. See," he went on excitedly, "I know a god-awful lot of junkies and most of them bring news around—sometimes free, sometimes for pay. I'll get all that I can for free, then we decide what we want to buy—"

"I decide."

"Okay, you decide. Anyway, we find out everything we can about Grey, then my part's done." He folded his good arm over his cast triumphantly.

I was touched. "That seems like a lot. You'll do this for some help and how much money?"

He began innocently. "Oh, I figured around a hundred sev—" He caught my eye and scowled. "Okay, okay, no money, if that's the way it's gotta be."

I said wonderingly, "A cokie who can turn it on and off. A panhandler who works for free. Joe, if you can do those things, you can do anything."

"Yeah, but I gotta want to awful bad." He stared ahead in silence, not focusing on anything. He had a nasty look to him, one he hadn't had before.

I didn't bother thinking about it. "It's a deal. Now, do you know the names of the two guys yet?"

He sagged. "Nope. They pop up once in a while when someone's taken out a loan or started selling for themselves; then they leave again. What I'm going to do, see, is since I know this guy who owes his dealer a couple C's and can't cough up, I'm going to tail him around till they beat him up, then I'll tail them. Maybe you can help find who they are and who they work for."

"How much did you owe?"

"None of your business." He put a hand on the cast. "Too much, I guess."

I thought about that. "Pretty efficient, using you to warn me. What do you know about these two?"

He shook his head. "Just what I told you before, I think. Oh—did I tell you one of them, the short one, had a gold tooth and gold tiepin? And he dresses flashy."

"How could you see his tiepin? You met him in-doors?"

"No, no. But he had his coat unbuttoned, and he wears his tiepin high enough so it shows that way." His lip curled. "I can't see why he'd bother."

"I didn't think you would."

He grinned amiably at me. "You're pretty fussy, ain't you? I bet you wash your hands before and after you pee." He cackled.

"Sometimes I even wash them during. Now get out for a while so I can do some work." He left, saying he'd drop back in when he found anything. This time I did sweep after he left.

I thought about his offer. It was a small break, but I needed a break badly. Since it seemed appropriate now, and since I'd been planning on it, anyway, I called up Reedy Rentschler's office.

The girl who answered sounded like she lived in velvet. There wasn't a sound behind her, not a whisper. "Rentschler Imports," she said, not even snickering.

"Could I speak to Randolph Rentschler, please?" I tried to sound harassed. "This is, uh, Phillips. Put me through quick; I haven't got much time and I won't get another chance to call. I'll take respon-sibility for being put through."

She said, suddenly formal, "I'm very sorry, but Mr. Rentschler is busy just now. Could you please call back in an hour?"

I said grimly, "I'm only allowed one phone call."

"Oh." She added quietly, "I'll get him right away."

She kept her word. In less than a minute I heard a whisper so dry it made my own throat hurt. "Yeah? Rentschler here. Grabotte? What happened?"

"This isn't Grabotte," I said quickly. "It's—"

"Then why the hell should I care if you're in the can or not?"

"You don't—" I cut back in "—but you might care about your business when something big happens to your competition."

That didn't stop him. "You got something to say, or you just throwing a scare at me?"

"I'm Nathan Phillips. I'm a private detective, but I worked on the Grogan murder case. Maybe you know me from that."

"You're in the phone book," he said indifferently. "You just call to be wise, or what?"

"I'm not being wise." That was true; this was one of the dumber things I'd ever done. "I'm still working on finding Grey. I don't suppose you like that."

"No. No, I don't. And I don't think you will, either."

"Maybe not, but I'd like to talk to you in person. When could I see you?"

There was a short silence. "There's probably a way to do this that takes less time, but I'm an agreeable man. How fast can you get here—you know where I am, right?"

"You're in the phone book." I hung up.

I was at the HCR building in ten minutes. He was forty-odd floors up in the tower, somewhere between the peasants and God. The office had just enough wood in it to make you realize it was ritzy, not enough to make you think it was cheap paneling. The chairs were soft and velvety, and there were thick green curtains that hung half open on a floor-to-ceiling window. The receptionist was long-haired, very blond, very pretty and she didn't like me.

"He'll see you," she said crisply when I showed

my card. She dropped the card in her decorator wastebasket.

I fished it out and chided her. "Those cards cost almost three cents apiece, you know." She smiled coldly. "Don't laugh; my overhead's lower than yours."

"Everything of yours is a little lower than ours." Her voice was as cold as her looks. "Cheap, window peeking, disgusting little—"

"My, what a loyal little employee you are. I suppose the boss lets you in on everything?" I glanced at her hands; she pulled them under her desk but not before I saw the wedding ring. I looked at her nameplate. "Yes, he really did let you in on everything."

She glared furiously and stood up; we were only a few feet apart. The door behind her opened, and I looked inside quickly. A potbellied man in his early fifties walked in and said in a husky whisper, "You like my wife, do you?"

She sat, patting her hair. I said, "Sure, I like her—but she's trying to convince me she's dangerous, and I'm convinced."

He laughed. It was a cheerful sound, a sort of hiss—like a kettle boiling. Years ago, someone must have hit him good and hard in the throat. He probably got a raspy voice and a nickname at the same time—and he learned to fight with his chin tucked after that.

"Don't stand there talking, Phillips, come on in." He held the door. I stepped by him and looked around.

His window overlooked the lake parks—Harriet, Calhoun, Lake of the Isles and the rest; it must have been a panorama of green and blue in the spring. Even in late winter the bare trees and dirty ice in the distance were desolately beautiful. I thought of sitting up here on winter afternoons, watching storms roll in from the west in the dying light.

"Yeah," he rasped, "it's a good view. I ought to know; I pay for it. Now sit the hell down and talk business."

"You really make me feel at home," I complained. "No small talk?"

"Business with you is small talk."

There was a snicker from the other door of the office. I'd thought it was a closet door. I spun around but remembered to keep my hand outside my suit coat.

Rentschler looked irritated. "I didn't want to introduce you, but I might just as damn well." He turned and knocked on the door. "Come on out, dummy."

The door opened and a pale watery-eyed man peered out. "Sorry." The door slammed.

"I hope he's better than that at something, or whatever he's paid is too much." I sat down.

Rentschler said, "He's a lot better at something, and I still pay him too much. Will you get to business?"

"I didn't stall us, your goon did. And if you want to talk business, I'll talk." I crossed my legs, taking care not to kick the oak desk in front of me. "I'm finding Grey, or I'm finding out what happened to him. You don't want me to find out, right?"

"I say you're not going to, and that's the truth." Nothing subtle in this office, from the secretary on up.

"Suppose I keep on looking?"

"This is a rough city. You could get hurt—maybe killed, maybe just beat up."

"I could get my arm broken in two places."

He didn't react. "If you want. Or—I tell you what. I'm reasonable. I can be mean, but it's bad for business. I could hire you for a month or two to read magazines for me; I'm too busy to read much. You understand?" He smiled, like an old man offering candy to a crying child.

I smiled back. "My client has money, too. I already accepted that money. Giving it back would be bad for my own business; you know that."

I annoyed him as much as I sometimes annoyed Jon Pederson. Rentschler opened drawers and peered under papers in a frenzy. "I hate talking with guys like you." He sounded like his throat was lined with gravel. "You never talk sense." He found what he was looking for—a bottle of antacid tablets—and spilled them on the desk, scooping up three or four, popping them in his mouth all at once and chewing furiously. "Now look, Phillips," he mumbled, puffing little white powder-clouds out in front of him, "you can't tell me it's too late to quit. You haven't even found anything out yet."

"You'd be surprised. The little I've got is enough to hurt your business."

He didn't like that at all. "Talk." This time his whisper was intentional.

I sat back, thinking. I wanted to get everything in the right order. "Number one: you didn't kill Grey, or keep him salted away, or anything." He looked at me in astonishment. "Anyone could figure that out. If Grey died, the Twin Cities drug market would see the bloodiest battle for control since Capone taught Chicago free enterprise. Especially if nobody's ready for Grey's disappearance. You with me so far?" He nodded.

"Naturally," I went on, "you don't want a drug war here. It would be—"

"Bad for business." Right on cue.

"Right. Which leads to number two: the longer Grey isn't around but isn't known to be dead, the better chance you have of getting all his business for yourself.''

"What do you mean?" There was hard suspicion in his soft voice.

"I mean—" I stopped and cleared my own throat "—that you're sure enough something happened to Stiff Grey that you're getting ready now for the scramble when the rest of the big-time dealers clue in. Everybody knows Rosetti could compete against gunmen, but he never ran a business like Grey's by himself. You figure if you can solidify your holdings and start edging in, then by the time the others decide Grey is permanently gone there won't be anything left to grab. That's why you're worried about an investigation just now, before you're ready. That's one reason, anyway. The other 'reason' called you a couple of days ago."

He didn't say anything, but glanced toward the door where his man was waiting. That didn't bother me. "And you'll lose a lot of guys like your closet friend, if I find out enough to make the other dealers even mildly interested."

He came around the desk and sat on it in front, staring at me earnestly. "Let me try to explain this so you'll understand. I wouldn't bother with you— you know that—but I got to protect my business. See these?" He fumbled around behind him on the desk and pulled out two pictures of men in their early twenties.

"These are my sons—smart boys, both of them. Dwight and Arnie. They were gonna go into this business, and they started with me about a year ago. I was hoping to turn it over to them some day." He slapped the pictures face down on the desk.

"It turns out they weren't good boys, just smart. They grew up during the hard times, the times when I got this—" he fingered his throat casually

"—and some scars. They thought that's the way to run a business, nothing but muscle and guns all the time. That only helps you keep a business, doesn't run it at all. Smart as they were, my kids couldn't figure that out. I was scared I'd have a world war on my hands before I got them out where they couldn't do any harm. They almost wanted to fight me, too—me, their father." He sighed. "If I was willing to kick my own sons out of my business to protect it, don't you think I'd be willing to take out a nosy detective I just met?"

"I suppose." I stopped. "But I'm willing to bet you won't unless you have to, because—" My own throat was hurting from listening to him. I leaned over in a coughing spasm; he hopped down and thumped my back for me. "Thanks. Because if you take me out too obviously, enough people will know you did it that one of them will wonder why you did. Then he'll find out what I was working on, and then he'll work on you, alone or with help, to make sure you don't take his cut of Grey's business." I got up. "It's been fun talking to you. Don't bother sending me any more broken arms; I'm a detective, not a doctor."

He found his voice—or at least the part he still had. "Just a minute, Phillips." He called out, "Okay, you two, step out."

From the next room came two men. One was good sized and flashily dressed, with flaming red hair and a mustache. The other, not as flashy, was the waxy-looking man I'd seen earlier; he was bigger than I'd expected, though not as large as his friend, and he wore a dull olive suit and a black tie. The only things colorful about him were his big gold ring—either he took it off for business or put on three more—and his gold tooth and tiepin. It was like Greasy to muddle their descriptions together. I smiled at them. Neither of them smiled back.

Rentschler said, "I don't think you'll get a chance to work on this guy, but in case you ever do, take a good look at him now. His name is Phillips, and he can't let well enough alone."

Flashy looked me over critically and said with vague, unsympathetic sadness, "That's a shame."

Gold Tooth said happily, "Maybe he could be taught." They turned and walked out, never looking back.

I turned back to Rentschler. "Do they sing and dance together, too?" Before he answered, I went on, "I've got a lot of work to do; so do you. I promise I'll let you know what I find out, even if I don't tell you till it's too late." While he sputtered I headed for the door but stopped and looked out the window again. "That really is beautiful. You ought to take time and look at it."

"I can't. I gotta keep paying for it."

I decided to ask. "I know the answer, I think, but do you remember anything about your last meeting with Grey that you think would help me?"

He didn't even laugh. "Get out." As a shout it would have been annoying; in that low hiss it was upsetting.

"Not yet. One more question: everyone else I've met thinks Stiff was a nice guy who had bad luck or who made his own bad luck. Why were all you thugs so scared of him?"

That stopped him. He scooped up another two antacids and chewed them briskly, without saying anything.

When he did talk he sounded subdued. "I don't know—but I think it was because you took one look at him and knew that here was a guy who didn't give a damn. He was willing to talk to you or shoot

you, and it didn't matter to him if you talked back
or shot back. It was all the same to him; I can't
think of anyone in the business who wasn't afraid
of him." He scowled. "Isn't, I mean." I didn't say
anything. "They're still scared—how else could he
disappear for two years and still not have anyone
take over his business?"

I couldn't answer that, so I left. On the way out I
told the receptionist, "I hate to break the bad news,
but he isn't having me shot."

"I'm heartbroken," she said icily. "I already vol-
unteered for the job."

"I'm leaving. I feel unloved."

When I got outside, a light stinging snow was driving through the downtown streets. It blew over the
pavement in faint little ghosts of waves. I headed
back to my office to think but gave up when I got
there and took my work home. I'd had all the trouble I needed for a while, and in stormy weather I'd
rather be home with hot tea on the stove and a
warm black cat in and out of my lap. I ate a late
lunch, then listened to the wind and read myself to
sleep over the printouts again.

I woke up at four-thirty and wrote down everything I had learned that had helped me. It fit on a
three-by-five index card, and most of it was questions. I picked up the phone automatically; I'd finished dialing before I caught myself. I hung up
quickly, though I could have let it ring; Mrs. Cartley
wouldn't be there to answer. Teach me to sleep in
the afternoon.

I tossed the card aside and spent the evening
reading dull books and telling Marlowe he didn't
really want to go outside. I was more convincing
talking to Rentschler.

7

I'D SEEN PROFESSOR DAVIES, and I'd talked at length to Harry and to Rentschler. That left one person to talk to, and if she didn't come through, I'd be pretty well stuck. The only other person who might know Grey's whereabouts besides her was Rosetti, and I didn't feel like asking him.

So, at five-thirty on a Friday afternoon, with a morning's fruitless legwork on a divorce case and an afternoon's hopeless office time behind me, I went over to Hennepin Avenue to find Deirdre Ryan. The weather, with one of those perverse April twists, was warmer again. It was slightly damp but well above freezing, and there was very little wind. The regular streetwalkers would be out; if I looked long enough, I'd find her.

Finding a whore on Hennepin Avenue is harder than finding a stoplight and easier than finding a parking place. Finding a particular whore, especially when you don't know what she looks like, is another matter. I parked on a side street, then wandered around the corner.

I walked about five feet before I met a woman with jet-black (probably dyed) hair, wet glossy lipstick and enough mascara to supply Academy Awards night. She had on a great-looking winter coat, but her handbag and shoes were both battered. Streetwalkers in good coats aren't rich; they just invest their profits wisely. Minneapolis street corners in the cold months make even the whores look warm.

I nodded to her. "Nice evening."

She sized me up and said with a mechanical tease in her voice, "Could be warmer."

"Maybe." She got out a cigarette; I lit it for her. (Always carry matches when you ignore your mother's advice and talk to strange women.)

"Thanks. Can't you do better than 'maybe'?" She took a long drag on the cigarette and stared down her heavy black lashes at me. With that much mascara, it was surprising she could see me.

"I'm trying to do better than 'maybe.' I'm looking for somebody named Deirdre Ryan; we have a friend in common."

She pouted, not too convincingly. "What has she got that I don't have?"

I leered, also not too convincingly. "My money, if I find her."

She looked at me suspiciously. "Dee's been jumpy about something for quite a while. You wouldn't know anything about that, would you, mister?"

I acted surprised. "Me? No, I just heard about her from a friend; he said I ought to meet her sometime." I decided it wouldn't hurt to act simple. "What's she look like, anyway? He didn't tell me."

"Flaming red hair. Green eyes." She pretended she was thinking. "That's about all I can remember." She took another drag, coughed raggedly. "All hookers look alike, even to hookers."

"Tsk. You shouldn't say things like that; you'll spoil the mood."

"What mood?" she answered sourly. "You're just wasting my time, and it's odds on—" she looked me up and down coldly "—you'll waste Dee's, too. You don't look like a cop or a pimp, but you don't look like a john, either."

"All right," I said. "I'm no customer. I've got some questions and I'm looking for a girl with some answers. Maybe two girls, if you can tell me where Deirdre Ryan is." I moved my hand toward my pocket, watching her reaction.

She bit. "Expensive questions?"

"No," I admitted. "Cheap ones. Where does she hang around, nights?"

"How cheap?"

"Two."

"Ten."

"Five."

She thought for a moment. "All right," she said finally. "She'll be in front of Henley's Bar and Restaurant in about twenty minutes. We always go there for a break."

"Hell, I could have found that out by waiting right here. I didn't get my money's worth."

Her lips curled. "I've heard that before."

I sized her up the way she had me. "I can't believe that," I said solemnly.

"Thanks. Look me up when you're not busy. What about my five?"

I reached in my pocket, began to extract my wallet. She glanced sideways and made a quick gesture to wait. "Not now. Turn your back to the street, take the money out with your matchbook and slip it to me."

I did as she said, palming the bill and passing it to her as I lit another cigarette for her. She shifted the cigarette to her other hand and pocketed the bill deftly. "Why did we go through that little charade?" I asked.

"Because," she said nastily, "that little old man across the street pays too much attention."

I looked, casually. He was wearing a seedy-looking overcoat and a flattened cap that did nothing to cover his ears, which stuck out far enough to flap in the wind.

"Looks more like an eavesdropper than a spy. Who is he?"

She snickered. "We call him Elephant Ears. He works for the vice squad, but what he mostly does is catch us between clients and shake us down for money, or else he'll haul us in."

"He couldn't have stuck you for what you just did."

"No." She blew smoke toward him disdainfully. "But tonight's a work night, and I can't afford the hassle. He knows that."

"Sounds like a pretty cheap racket."

"It is. If he likes taking money from us, why doesn't he just become a pimp?" She sounded genuinely puzzled.

"He likes to think he's in an honest profession," I answered. "To some people the thought is comforting."

She looked at me to see if I were serious, then looked disgusted. "That's really warped." She shook her head. "The things some people will do." She pulled her coat tighter around her and brushed at her eyes as a passing bus blew dust in them.

"Yeah. Easy, you'll smear your mascara. See you at the café." I walked on up the street to Henley's. It was a regular bar and restaurant, not a fancy place or a tough one. The King of Spain wasn't likely to come for dinner, but neither was Barnacle Bill the Sailor. I waited outside. The ordinary pedestrians looked at me curiously, the streetwalkers speculatively. Everybody passed me by.

All at once a girl stopped in front of me. She wore less makeup than a streetwalker, but her coat was too heavy for someone who wasn't working the street. Her face looked as though she'd been hooking since age twelve. She just stood there, eyeing me.

"Well," I said finally, "what do you want? I can't stand the suspense."

She glared at me, held her handbag open in front of her and said in a demanding nasal voice, "Will you give a few dollars to the Reformed Higher Hindu Consciousness Church of Bloomington?"

I nearly laughed in her face. "Sorry, I gave all my money to the Fund for the Venetian Blind."

She didn't get mad, just shook her handbag a couple times, inviting my wallet to jump in. "Your contributions make greater spiritual consciousness a certainty. Will you please contribute?" Her tone implied I'd be in serious trouble if I didn't.

I was going to tell her to shove off when I noticed Elephant Ears watching dubiously from around the corner of the building. She rattled her handbag once more and said impatiently, "Well, will you or won't you?" Elephant Ears looked less dubious.

I decided to remove all doubt from my mind. I folded up a bill—it was only a one, and I wanted to make sure he couldn't see that—and dropped it visibly and carefully into her purse. I gave her my best leer. "It's been swell doing business with you."

She snapped her handbag shut and moved off down the street in search of better pickings. The old man followed, speeding up to overtake her.

I wanted to watch the fun, but another woman came up. This was my night.

She had red hair, green eyes and a slender build. Her coat was tailored to show off that build—warmth and advertising in one. She had long nervous fingers that crossed and uncrossed; the nails were bitten. Besides looking cold, and at the most a hard twenty-two, she looked just a little afraid of me.

She said in a surprisingly warm voice, "Sara said you wanted to talk."

"Do I owe her for that, too? I had to pay to find out where you were."

"It was a favor. Don't take it personally; she was warning me, not helping you." She glanced in the café window. So did I; the reflection showed no one watching us.

"Deirdre Ryan?" I asked. She nodded. "I'm a private investigator, and I'd like to ask you some questions."

Her eyes narrowed, and she all but hissed, "If you're trying to buy something on one of my—"

I waved a hand at her. "Take it easy. I didn't say that was what I wanted. As long as we're talking, let's do it inside. I'll buy you a drink, or a cup of coffee or even some ice cream, and you don't have to answer any questions you don't want to. Is it a date?"

Her eyes got an odd faraway look in them. "A date?" Suddenly she grinned. "Okay, it's a date." I opened the door for her and she went through first, looking suddenly self-conscious and shy.

We made our way past the cashier, an Italian with dark wavy hair and arched eyebrows; he bowed quickly to both of us as though we were royalty. We took a table for two near the back. It wasn't much protection from being seen—the place was too small for that kind of privacy—but at least it might keep us from being interrupted. I held out her chair; she blushed as she sat down, and thanked me.

I ordered two cups of coffee. While we studied the menus I said, "I bet you're dying to know what I'm up to."

"You're right. Know what? I've never had an escort to this place before." She stared around as though it was all new and different.

"If I'd known what I was getting into, I'd have worn a boutonniere." She giggled nervously, but subsided as I added, "And now to the business at hand."

"Not yet. First, who are you working for?" She picked up a spoonful of sugar and put it in her coffee, carefully brushing the stray grains off the rim into the cup.

"I'm working for a client whose name I can't reveal, and I have the backing of the police—easy, easy!"

She was getting up. "Putting the pinch on my... clients is worse than squeezing them. I—"

"I'm not doing either. Though I bet we could agree on a price." She looked at me coldly, but I had her thinking. "But I'm not blackmailing anyone today." She nodded, and just for a moment she looked disappointed. "As a matter of fact, I may be saving your life or one of your customers'."

She sat up straight at that, and looked over my shoulder quickly. I studied the barroom mirror for a moment, picking out the place's other clientele. They looked pretty mild mannered to me. Whatever else Deirdre was, she was good and nervous, and someone was keeping her that way.

My first question didn't help her. "Didn't you phone in a complaint about a john sometime last November?"

"What if I did?" She picked up a spoon and stirred her coffee violently. "I dropped it. He wouldn't pay me, and then he decided to, that's all."

"Come off it, Miss Ryan. You were in Stiff Grey's house—Benny Rosetti's residence, these days. Neither of them would bother welshing on your fee unless they intended to stick to it for some reason. If they decided to stick, the police couldn't pry them loose. What happened?"

"What makes it your business?" Her voice was querulous, tension filled. She'd been living with strain for some time.

I broke out my worried tough-guy imitation. "Look, lady, I'm only trying to make sure there isn't any trouble. Maybe you need some protection."

She picked up her coffee, put it to her lips and set it down hastily. "Maybe I need Fort Snelling and two platoons." She ran a finger over her burned lips. Her nails were bitten to the quick and below.

I said reassuringly, "So you must know something Rosetti, or Grey, doesn't want spread around. I work pretty closely with the police on this; if either Rosetti or Grey did something we could nail them for, you could stop worrying about them out there, waiting."

She shuddered. There was a noise at the door; we both looked quickly. A group of eight or nine streetwalkers came in, talking and laughing. The cashier practically fell off his little stool waving at them and rolling his eyes, flirting with them. They giggled and waved back, then sat down, gossiping like junior-high girls.

One of them noticed the two of us sitting together and whispered to the others, pointing us out. I said to Deirdre, "You're in for it now." She blushed. Somebody once told me my manners would make a hooker blush, but I don't think this was what he had in mind.

"Just ignore them and we'll talk," she said in a low voice.

"I'll ignore them, but you'll have to talk; I don't have much to say. You went to Grey's address last November—I'd guess because Rosetti came and got you."

"How do you know he didn't phone or send someone?'' She tried her coffee again, looking at me suspiciously over it.

"Stands to reason. You'd be hard to get by phone, and neither of those two thugs would have someone else pick out a girl for them,'' I said, picking up my coffee cup and watching her over it for a reaction. "And these days that kind of work isn't in Grey's line.'' Did she know whether or not Grey was alive?

She shivered and laughed nervously, not a nice laugh at all. "No, it isn't. You're right, there; it certainly isn't.''

She gulped down some coffee and made a face. She threw another heaping teaspoon of sugar in and stirred, making the spoon clatter.

I prompted her, "Are you going to tell me?''

"No.'' She said it in a small voice.

I asked coaxingly, to match her little-girl voice, "Do you want some ice cream or maybe a piece of pie?''

She smiled then. "I'd like that,'' she said slowly, "but look, I'm not a lost kid at the circus. Get me a piece of apple pie, but it won't make me talk.''

"Bets?'' I signaled a waiter and got two pieces of apple pie. When he left I added, "Then if you won't talk, I will. I might have known you wouldn't trust me; I've known since I saw you you didn't have any judgment.''

"How do you know?'' She looked hurt.

"You ever heard of a girl crazy enough to get picked up by a coked-up gunman?''

"He wasn't high that night,'' she snapped. She picked up her napkin and began tearing it into small strips.

"You're not telling me he was in his right mind,'' I sneered. "He wouldn't have showed you what he did if he was.''

It was a risk, but not much of a one; it paid off,

but only a little. "He wouldn't have shown me anything, coked," she said. "He was drunk. He was
very drunk, somewhere between dancing on tables
and tripping over shadows. He's...different when
he's drunk. They say cocaine makes him mean,
hard; liquor makes him...generous." She finished
off the napkin and put another teaspoon of sugar in
her coffee without tasting it. "I knew who he was,
and I didn't want to go with him, but I was afraid
not to. And he offered me a hundred bucks for half
an hour." She stared into space.

"So you went with him."

She nodded. "So I went with him."

"What did you do?" She looked at me pityingly.
"Okay, dumb question. What happened then?"

"He paid me, and then he started to laugh." Her
voice faded until I thought it would go out completely.

"Then what?"

"He kept laughing, and he—he told me he had a
friend."

"What did you say?"

"I said, sure, if the price is right. Rosetti just kept
laughing. Then he led me upstairs—" She stopped,
biting her lip.

"And?"

She shook her head. "I ran out. Behind me I could
hear him laughing, loud and crazy. I thought I heard
him all the way home." She sipped at her coffee,
frowned and put still another half teaspoon of sugar
in. It looked like syrup already. "I was pretty cautious the next day, nervous and jumpy; I lost a lot of
business.

"When I got home late that night I had fifty dollars and a long-stemmed rose in my mailbox. No
note and no name. It had to be from Rosetti, telling
me to keep my mouth shut."

I said impatiently, "So what did you see?"

She looked across at me, her lips drawn tight. "Thanks for the coffee and the pie." She didn't get up, though, and she didn't look like she wanted to keep it to herself.

I said casually, "I don't suppose you know what Grey looks like."

"No. I don't think I've ever seen him." She put just enough emphasis on "think" to make me wonder.

"Nobody's seen him for some time," I persisted. "Some people say Rosetti took care of him. From what I've heard of Rosetti I'll bet that if he did, he took care of Grey good."

"You can bet on that." She shivered again. She took a sip of her coffee. "God, this is bitter."

"Lady, if it were any sweeter, it'd jump up and kiss you on the cheek. I guess you don't want to say any more, do you?" She shook her head. "That's all right. I can understand why you're scared. You look like you could use a friend."

"I'll be okay." She smiled weakly. "Lots of people look that way. You do."

"What?"

"Look like you could use a friend, I mean. It shows in your face."

"I have friends enough." I changed the subject back. "Well, if you want to talk or need help, call."

She looked confused and embarrassed. "I forgot to ask your name."

I grinned. "Guess it's not a habit you'd get into." I took out my card, crossed out my partner's name and said, "That's me. Anytime you want to talk, call. I'll listen." I wrote my home phone number on the back while I said, "I'm trying to find Stiff Grey; he's been missing for two years. If Rosetti did get him two years ago, I don't suppose there's much left by now."

She looked faraway and fumbled for her gloves. "I wouldn't think so." She was hardening again, getting ready to go outside.

I leaned forward. "If—"

That was as far as I got. The old man with the flapping ears ran up to our table, red as a badly boiled lobster and twice as disagreeable. "You the smartass that was talking to the religious nut out front?"

Everyone was watching us. I cleared my throat. "You mean the kid taking donations?"

"That's the one, you smartass! I saw you with her."

"Don't tell my mother."

One of the girls watching us giggled. He choked and said angrily, "You set me up, you little smartass. You set me up."

I said innocently, "All I did was give a dollar to spread higher spiritual consciousness."

Baffled frustration shook his dried-up cheeks. "It wasn't even a five. I spent ten minutes working on her."

"That's nice. Did it do your soul any good?"

All the girls laughed then. Elephant Ears muttered, "Smartass" one last time, stuffed his ridiculous hat above his ridiculous ears and stomped out.

One of the girls signaled the waiter and whispered. He hurried to the cashier and whispered to him, then ran to the back.

The cashier ran over excitedly and far from whispered to me, "You are very lucky, very lucky, mister. The ladies here, they have ordered you a hot-fudge sundae and paid for it." He waved his arms. "This has never happened here before."

"It's not that exciting," I growled, but I turned to the girls, nodded and waved. They giggled and ducked their heads, and they giggled again as the waiter came running out with the sundae.

I said to Deirdre, "Care to join me? You can use your coffee spoon."

She looked wistfully at it. "No, thank you. I've got to get back to work. Besides, I can't eat ice cream very often—too fattening. None of us can; that's why the others gave you a sundae, to show it was a special occasion. The apple pie was more than enough for me."

. I looked at her face, still wistful over the ice cream but hardening with thoughts of going back to work, and drawn with worry. Suddenly I reached across, grabbed her spoon and filled it with ice cream and hot fudge. "At least take the first bite," I said coaxingly. "It's a special occasion." I held it across to her at mouth level.

She looked at me blankly for a second, then broke into a smile that maybe used to belong on her face but hadn't in years. She pulled off her right glove and guided the spoon into her mouth, careful not to touch my hand. She was blushing again. "Thanks." I helped her with her coat, and she left for the street. The other girls followed quickly.

I ate the sundae slowly, savoring the hot fudge and thinking of hard young women who flirt with cashiers and gossip during coffee breaks. I also thought long and hard about Rosetti and what he could have shown Deirdre. If it had been Grey's corpse, it would be pretty ripe by now. And if Grey was dead—I put down my spoon. The police print-out had listed checks to Grey's account in the past two years. Who had signed them?

I paid for the coffee and the pie, then offered the cashier a few dollars to pay for the girls' next break. He waved it away. "I pay for the ladies' first cup myself, always." He thumped his chest and beamed. He leaned over the cash register as though imparting a great secret. "Nice ladies, eh?"

"You bet." I pulled on my stocking cap and went out.

I passed one of them on the street. She nodded and looked away. Off hours were done; the night was still warm, but the cashier's ladies were cold again.

8

SATURDAY I let everyone else alone and they let me alone. I sat at home watching old movies and trying to keep my sandwiches away from Marlowe. I unjacked the phone and left a piece of junk mail in my mailbox so no one would think I was home. I feel like that at the end of a long Minnesota winter anyway; I've often wished I could hibernate.

By the middle of Sunday afternoon, however, I was restless. None of the sports broadcasts on TV appealed to me—if it's past Vikings season, and the Twins aren't playing, what is there left—and I'd had my fill of movies. Even Marlowe could feel it; he stalked across my lap, making discontented noises and digging his claws into my trousers.

So I let him out and went for a walk. The sky was a dull gray; it was the kind of weather that just hangs overhead looking dismal. I headed up to Lake Street and a grocer I knew who stocked good meat even on weekends. Not an exciting walk, but it beat what I'd been doing with my time.

I paid for my groceries by check, feeling flattered when the cashier said he didn't need to see my ID. As I walked across the parking lot I heard somebody panting behind me, "Wait!" I turned around.

He ran up. "God, you're hard to catch up with. Can't you have those legs taken in?"

"Tailors are so expensive. Catch your breath, Bernie."

He waved a hand and bent forward like a jogger doubling up after five miles. He couldn't have run more than half a block. "You're hard to find, too."

"Not by phone."

"I should have thought of that. No, wait; it wouldn't have done any good. Dave Komarek tried to call you; you weren't ever in."

"What did he want? I just saw him—"

"Two weeks ago. It's been two weeks; that's long for you. How are you doing?"

"Me? Oh, fine, fine. You?"

He thought a moment. "I'm engaged."

We started walking again. "I have been out of touch, haven't I? Just a week ago you weren't even in love. Congratulations. When are you breaking it off?"

He scuffed at the curb aimlessly. "Oh, I don't know. Couple weeks, I guess. The announcement isn't even out yet." He grinned and brushed the hair out of his eyes. Bernie's as charming as a sheep-dog pup. With his hobby he'd have to be. "You're walking too fast."

"You're going to stay with her till after her showers, right? Thoughtful of you." We slowed down. "Nice girl?"

"Woman. Wooo-mannn. Show some respect."

"My mistake. Bernie, half of them haven't even been nineteen. Older this time?"

"Twenty-seven, twenty-eight." He added slyly, "You used to go out with her."

"You're joking. Who?" He told me. "Sherri? Sherri's engaged to you?"

He said stiffly, "Why not? She'd already gone out with you; how much lower could she stoop?" He sighed. "It's a little different from my other engagements, Nate. She hopes if I meet her family and 'break her heart,' her grandmother will get off her back about getting married.''

I nodded. ''Seems like a waste of everybody's time. Sherri's happy single. How does it feel to be so constructive while you're having fun?''

He hesitated, then said puzzledly, ''Not good. I don't know why, either. It's not like I'm a bastard the rest of the time.'' Which was true: his engagements were whirlwind, his breakups gentle and apparently mutual, and he was still on friendly terms with most of the girls—women—he'd jilted.

''I think it's the first time you've had to take any of this seriously, Bernie. God love you, you'd hate that.''

''Maybe you're right.'' He skidded on a patch of ice in the shadow of a building. ''Pity you're not doing this one yourself. You're much better at taking things seriously.''

''What's so bad about that?''

''Nothing. Nothing. Forget it.'' He changed the subject. ''What Dave probably called you about, Nate, is we've got a poker game coming up next Wednesday. Wondered if you'd like to come.'' He saw me hesitating and added, ''Low stakes.''

I laughed. ''I figured when you said Dave was in on it. How'd you get him to play cards, anyway? He takes things even more seriously than I do.''

I was baiting him and he knew it. He pushed the hair out of his eyes again and said, ''Not really. He just looks more serious than you do. It's that Eurasian face with the big sad eyes. He could look worried after winning a bet. Nate, are you okay?''

''What?''

''How 'bout that—I finally got you to stop walk-

ing. Are you okay? I know you haven't had the
world's easiest nine days."

"Nine days? What...?" Right. Roy had been
dead about nine days. "No. No, I haven't. I'm doing
all right, though. Don't worry about it."

"Taking it well, are you?"

"I'm fine."

"Nate, you can poke fun at my engagements and
tell me I don't take things seriously enough, but
don't ever give me that kind of crap." He looked
puzzled and annoyed. "I'm not doing this right. I
knew I wouldn't do this right. How come I'm so
great at proposing and I can't do a simple thing like
talk to a friend?"

"Forget it, Bernie. I can't, either."

He shook his head. "You can't because you're so
serious about people. I ought to be able to. What I'm
trying to say is, you don't have to want to go out
and have a good time; just call us. You need to be
around people, to—"

"I know what I need." He looked hurt. "Sorry,
Bernie. I'm lousy at this. Maybe that's why I
haven't called anybody; I know I'd just get nasty.
You're a hell of a nice guy, and I'll be by. Sometime
soon. You'll see."

"Don't wait till you feel better," he said, and I'd
never seen him look more earnest. "We like you
just as much when you're a jerk."

"You could put that better."

He grinned. "Even Sherri likes you when you're a
jerk. She told me about the first time you went out.
Remember? Some woman whose husband had hired
you to tail his wife years ago came to your table
stinking drunk and—"

"I can't believe Sherri told you about that. I'm
just glad nobody took pictures."

"That's what you think. Next time we get togeth-

er, maybe Sherri can show the slides." He slapped
my arm. "I've got to get back to my car. It's full of
groceries; I forgot to lock it."

"Bet they've been ripped off."

He shrugged. "Happens. Oftener than it should,
to some of us. Take care, Nate."

"So long—and I will call. It may be a while, but I
will."

"Call Dave, will you? I'm never home. Besides,
you've got to plan my bachelor party."

"Not another one. I'm still half hung over from
your last one." He laughed and left. I walked home
wondering what had just happened and how I felt
about it.

I should have been pleased, or else annoyed. My
life was none of his business, and I should have
been flattered that he'd made it his. Somehow I
didn't feel any of that yet. I like living alone; I'm
used to doing things alone. Sometimes in a situation
where I could turn to my friends, I won't. Not right
away.

But I was pretty sure that in a few weeks, maybe
more, I'd know how to feel about his offer. Probably I'd even call him or Dave. For now, even that
meager certainty was a help. I went back home and
took the junk mail in and rejacked the phone and
fed my cat. Cats don't care how good or how bad
you feel as long as you feed them. They're annoying
that way. Sometimes they're good that way.

9

NEXT MONDAY MORNING my office was dead quiet. I stayed there till ten waiting for business. I might as well have been waiting for a ski lift in Kansas. I got some more filing done and reread my fact sheet on Stiff Grey.

I'd done enough checking on whom he saw and what he did; it hadn't helped me. Nothing much had changed in two years; there was little new to find. I decided to change things—see if I could develop something new. I started with Grey's personal checks.

They were all drawn on the same account at the Minneapolis-St. Paul Security Bank. The amounts of the checks were listed. I don't know how the police got those without a fight. Maybe they didn't.

After a little looking I figured out that Grey's "personal checking account" was a money laundry; in two years, more than three million dollars had gone through it. Grey was following a great American tradition; the syndicate heads had been pushing money through their family members' personal accounts since the fifties. Grey was playing a little closer to the chest than they had, though; he was using his own checking account, and possibly his savings account, to clean money for other operators. Probably he was getting his own money cleaned elsewhere in exchange, but his system was a bit too direct. If anything went wrong, he'd be nailed to the wall.

After two hours of pencil sharpening I gave up. Grey was good; nothing ever went wrong. An account like Grey's had to have three things: careful depositors, no sinister relationships between entering funds and exiting funds, and enough cash on hand so that checks could flow through with no holdups and messy confirmation calls. Grey apparently had all three.

He might not keep the third ingredient forever, though; nearly a quarter of a million dollars had been transferred from his savings account and then withdrawn over the past two years. The checks went a lot of places, but ten of them, each for ten thousand dollars, went to Rosetti. In addition, there was an initial check to Rosetti for five thousand dollars. The checks to Rosetti were evenly spaced over the past twenty-two months.

I wondered idly what Rosetti's salary had been before Grey disappeared. My bet was that it had gone up a lot. That first five-thousand-dollar check bothered me. Even so, it was no stranger than the whole setup. If Grey was alive, why the checks? If Grey was dead, how the checks, and why withdraw the money so slowly?

I glanced at the report's description of Grey's checks. They sounded ordinary enough: typewritten except for the signature. The police, God knows how, had verified that the checks were typed on a model identical to one Grey had bought in 1975. The signature, the report said, was always Grey's and was never a rubber stamp. All of which was important without being helpful.

I toyed with the idea that somebody had always signed Grey's name for him in his business, but I gave up on it. If the police had bothered to look for

the typewriter, they'd have bothered to check
Grey's college signature against his recent ones.

I had a glimmering, then, and before it faded or
my nerve left me I looked up the number and
dialed. Right on the first ring a cheerful voice
answered, "Minneapolis-St. Paul Security."

"Hello. This is Nathan Phillips; is it possible to
speak to the bank's vice-president?"

Nothing but cheer on the other end. "Quite
probably, sir. We have several, however. Which
one do you want?"

"The one who deals with check frauds of fifty
thousand dollars or more."

It was quiet for a moment. Then she said, "Hang
on." All the cheerfulness was gone.

I waited, not more than a minute, rolling pencils
around my desk drawer. A new voice came on and
said with crisp authority, "This is Dawson Williams,
acting president of the bank. I understand you have
a serious complaint, Mr. Phillips."

I settled back. "Not at all, Mr. Williams—just a
routine investigation of one of your customers. I
thought it might save time if I were frank with your
receptionist."

"Perhaps." He sounded unhappy. "However, we
appreciate discretion in these matters. I hope you
don't make a habit of telling your business to anyone who answers the phone."

I laughed. "No, I don't. And I won't have to
again, now; I can just bring my business to you."

"I suppose." A little crisper now, like leaves
after a heavy frost. "At any rate, what do you
want?"

"I'd like to talk to you in person today, at your convenience. Ordinarily I'd be willing to wait days for
an appointment, but under the circumstances. . . ." I
trailed off.

"Just what are the circumstances, Mr. Phillips? You haven't said much that's definite."

"I won't over the phone, either. They may be a great deal worse than I suggested to your receptionist. May I come in today?"

I practically heard him licking his lips and checking his ulcer. "Naturally. Let me check." I heard papers rustle, then he said hastily, "I can see you between eleven and eleven-thirty this morning, Mr. Phillips."

"Fine," I said. "I'll be in." I started to hang up.

"Just a moment!" His reserve broke; he sounded very upset. "Who does this charge involve?"

"There are no formal charges yet," I said carefully. "And if you don't mind, I'd rather not say anything more over the phone. As you say, a little discretion is nice in these matters."

"Mmm. Goodbye, Mr. Phillips." He hung up. Quickly I dialed Jon Pederson's number at Homicide.

"Pederson? This is Nathan Phillips. Can you make sure that when a bank president calls the police about me he hears that my credentials are good and that I'm believed to be working on Stiff Grey's case?"

"What are you into now?"

"Nothing much. I just want to rattle the bank a bit, so they'll start bothering Rosetti. I want Rosetti jumpy, and a bank president can do it better than I can."

"You're right, there," he said heavily. "But if I were you, I wouldn't want anyone leaning on Benny Rosetti."

"I'm not worried." Much. "Can you see that the banker hears I'm all right?"

He sighed. "No problem. I've already asked that any and all calls from or concerning you be transferred to my department."

"You did?" That made me think. "You're that
certain there's going to be a murder involved?"

"It doesn't have to mean that. It might not even
be business." He coughed. "Let's just say I thought
I'd better keep track of you."

I didn't like that. "So much for my privacy. Anybody ever tell you this country was turning into a
police state?"

"Half the people I talk to," he said irritably. "You
got no call to talk that way, Nate. All right, I'll tell
the banker you're clean. Then I'll tell him you're
also a no-good, crazy, devious, cunning son—" I
hung up, straightened my tie, used my office shaver
and swiped at my shoes with a polishing cloth. I
wished, futilely, that I had a carnation for my lapel.

At 11:00 I walked in the front door of the
Minneapolis-St. Paul Security Bank, main office. It
was a nice building—a little like a courthouse, a little like the Pentagon and a little like the lobby of a
fancy motel. The walls were gray and bare. The
chairs were colorful and padded. The lighting was
stark and bright; the plants, mostly philodendrons,
were lush and dark. I felt like I was getting a warm
welcome to a fort.

Instead of barging right in, I waited to talk to one
of the tellers. I picked a tall thin fellow with a short
haircut, an elfish face and a goatee that looked like
it was standing in until the real beard came back
from the cleaners.

He was listening politely to an irritated old lady
with a shopping bag. "One dollar," she was saying,
shaking her head. "It's for one dollar. It's a small
enough risk for a big bank."

He shook his head tiredly; apparently, I'd joined
things after a long discussion. "Frankly, madam,"
he said in an accent as midwestern as Harvard, "the
bank doesn't care if you write it for one dollar or

one hundred; we still can't cash it unless it's drawn on a checking account here." He looked as though he wanted to add something biting, but he kept his temper.

She scowled. "Don't say 'can't,' damn ya! You know the bank can cash a one-dollar check if it wants."

"All right, if you want to be rude I may as well be, too; we won't. It's our policy, and I don't feel like breaking policy." He was bored and tired, and looked like he didn't belong here.

She rattled her paper bag at him. "Damn ya. You won't help, you won't bend the rules—what the hell kind of teller are you?"

"If I were a teller," he said stiffly, "I'd be an excellent one. Actually, I'm a Junior Subchief of Programming in Accounting, and I took this window to fill in for someone who is ill. All of which makes absolutely no difference to you or to your check."

She slammed her shopping bag down unexpectedly and wailed, "I don't have enough money for the buuuus! How am I going to get hooome?"

He looked at her sympathetically. "I'm really very sorry," he said kindly. "Isn't there something you could do?"

She looked at him blankly, and her right arm tensed. Before she could swing the bag at him, I stepped in. "I have a dollar, ma'am. Just let me fill in the name." I handed her the dollar and took the check she had half finished.

"Thank you so much. What a nice young man!" she said to nobody in particular. "How come you can afford to do this when a billion-dollar bank can't?"

"I have a better credit rating. Security Bank buys too many municipal bonds." The Junior Subchief was irritated by that crack but let it go. The old lady pinched my cheek, giggled and waddled off. I turned to the teller's window.

"Thank you very much, sir," the elf said happily. "There wasn't much I could have done for her."

I scratched my head. "You could have done what I did and cashed the check for yourself later."

He looked at me indifferently. "I suppose. However, I don't think it would be good policy for me, if it isn't for the bank."

"Maybe you're right. I bet you'll be glad to get back to Accounting."

"I'll be ecstatic." His eyebrows moved up and down with his voice. "I loathe this job. People."

"You work mostly with computers?"

"Almost entirely. Do you know, the thing I like best about machines is that if you tell them what to do and you tell them correctly, they'll do it. Machines never ask for exceptions."

I looked at him hard. "Maybe machines don't deserve them."

He looked at me blankly. "Not as much as she does?" He gestured at the door the old lady had left by.

"No, and not as much as you or I do."

He thought a moment. "If we all deserve exceptions, though, how can there be any at all? Exceptions are solely for the exceptional." He smiled at his own cleverness; for a moment he looked young and engaging and very, very proud.

I said, "Let's take an example, then. If anybody came in here to cash a ten-thousand-dollar check out of someone's account, and the anybody wasn't an account holder at the bank, what would he have to go through?"

He screwed up his forehead. "For a check that large there would be a lot of procedure, naturally. Probably the teller would take the check for approval to one of the vice-presidents or to the president. While the executive was looking at the account records, one of the accountants would call up the receiver's bank and make sure that there was enough in the receiver's account to refund the check without his having deposited the check itself, if there were any difficulty.''

"Does the bank have any legal right to the receiver's money in that situation?''

"You asked about procedures, not rights.''

"And procedure in this case is to lean on the receiver and thereby avoid legal difficulties and publicity for the bank. Handy, but is it ethical?''

He looked stubborn. "I don't know if it's ethical, either; it's policy.''

"Makes sense, I guess. What happens after the accountants phone the other bank?''

"Then,'' he said, "we go in and tell the president—or the vice-president—that there's enough in the receiver's account to cover the check.''

"You don't tell him how much there is over and above the amount of the check, do you?''

"Why, no,'' he said, startled. "That doesn't really matter, does it?''

"I guess not. Thank you for explaining all this. Policy is a fascinating thing. And now, would you please notify Mr. Williams that Mr. Phillips is here?''

He picked up a phone and spoke into it, then pointed toward a glass-and-chrome door behind me. "Go in there, sir.'' He looked down at his books and forgot about me completely.

I went to the door and pushed it open. The interior had shag carpet, overstuffed chairs, a set of Matisse watercolors and a desk the size of a handball court. Behind the desk, in a leather swivel chair, sat a middle-aged man who dressed like a

teenage executive and posed like an elder states-
man. His suit cut was imperially slim; his stomach
definitely wasn't. He had a modest tie whose effect
was spoiled by a huge silver-plate tiepin. He looked,
behind the hair dye and the stiffly majestic pose, to
be about forty or forty-five.

"Mr. Phillips," he said unhappily, "you'd best
come to the point quickly. Like any bank, we dislike fraud investigations, but we dislike frauds still
more. Tell me why you think there is a problem."

I passed my license over to him. He looked at it
briefly and handed it back. "When I called the
police," he said as if he'd never asked me anything,
"they informed me you were involved in a confidential matter and that you might appreciate our
assistance."

Pederson must have worded that himself; he
didn't quite lie and say it was police work. "I could
use your help. However, I came over today because
I wanted to offer help, not get it."

"Who are you working for in this matter—someone with a personal interest in the bank? Or perhaps—" he gestured as though it was unimportant,
but his eyes never left my face "—a law-
enforcement agency?"

"I'm afraid I can't say. What I can say, though," I
said as I leaned an elbow on his desk, "should interest you a great deal. About once every two months
or so, a Mr. Benny Rosetti cashes a check at this
bank for ten thousand dollars. It's always signed by
Steven Grey, and drawn on his account."

"Yes?" He didn't mean "yes," and he didn't
mean "no," but suddenly he was tense.

"Mr. Williams, no one has seen Steven Grey in
two years. Did it ever occur to you to have those
check signatures analyzed?"

He shifted uncomfortably. "Why, no. They

passed a cursory inspection, and we had no reason to insist on a more elaborate investigation. Mr. Grey has been drawing other checks on his account regularly during the last few years, and the checks to Rosetti seem no different than the others—except, of course, the amount." He coughed. "And to my knowledge, no one has ever questioned the checks' authenticity."

I thought of mentioning the police investigation of the checks, but why bother? Obviously, he had to know about it. "Grey's heirs might."

"His heirs?" he said, shocked. "You mean he might be dead now?"

"Worse—he might have died about eleven checks to Rosetti ago. That's $105,000. Of course, any other checks written to Grey's account during that time would be as fraudulent—but I imagine Rosetti got the most money from Grey's account."

Williams tried to smile but only looked strained. "Even supposing all this were true, Mr. Phillips, the checks were covered. We could regain the full amount without undue legal action or publicity. Each time Mr. Rosetti cashed a check of Grey's we phoned Rosetti's bank; his account could adequately cover any of the checks."

I sat back in the chair, crossing my legs. "Any, yes—but not necessarily all." The smile left. It wouldn't come back. "You had your people phone Rosetti's bank to see whether he had enough money for them to quietly refund each check if it was phony, without counting on the money he got for the check. I guess you feel that keeps you out of court—or the papers.

"Your people reported each time that Rosetti had enough to cover. The first time he only cashed a five-thousand-dollar check, maybe because he knew you'd look to see what he had, and he

couldn't cover a larger amount. He threw that
check in with his own money and kept just enough
in his known accounts to cover each subsequent
ten-thousand-dollar check. You forgot to ask if the
total covered by all those checks was there; my
guess is that if someone contests the signatures on
those checks, Rosetti's known accounts are about
ninety-five thousand dollars short."

Williams looked sick. "You say there's no trace of
most of the total?" he croaked.

"I don't really know. I'm guessing from things I
just learned this morning; I came over the minute I
knew."

He whirled to the phone, punched numbers frantically, then flipped a file index up from a desk
drawer. "Yes, this is Dawson Williams over at
Minneapolis-St. Paul Security. Could you give me
some figures on your accounts for—" he glanced
down quickly, "—Benito Rosetti, numbers 596-
57-2164, -5, and -6, please. You'll find my clearance
for this information on the list to the right of your
phone.... Yes, I'll wait." He tapped his foot
impatiently—and jumped a few seconds later.
"Hello? Yes? What? Thank you."

He scribbled frantically on the index card. "Do
you have any other accounts in Mr. Rosetti's name?"
He listened. "I see. Thank you very much." He
slammed down the phone and gasped, "My God, he
only has twelve thousand dollars!" He was ashen.

"He has more than that, if you could find that
much," I said cheerfully. "But he'll try to keep you
from finding the rest. It looks like he had something
to worry about on those other checks, doesn't it?"

Williams nodded, and he got an awful gleam in his
eye. "Of course, we could try to collect on anything
he's bought with that money."

"Only if he has clear title to those things—which

he probably knows," I said. "Probably most of his personal property is in Grey's name, even though Rosetti bought it; that way you'd be hard put to straighten out title. You'd be hard put to catch it fast enough, too. The house, the cars, the furniture—all of it could be converted to cash in a week if he wanted to badly enough, and all of it could be kept in Grey's name until the sale, ostensibly for Grey."

The bank president said grimly, "You don't seem terribly upset about this."

"I think it's funny that a bank that won't cash a check for a dollar from a little old lady would get bilked out of ninety-five thousand by a heavy co-caine user who doesn't have an account with it." He looked at me, and I quit smiling. "But I sympathize with you. That's why I came in this morning; I thought I'd warn you and give you some advice. You want to find out for sure if he has the money to cover those checks?"

"Of course," Williams answered impatiently, and twitched his right hand on the desk top.

"Then stop payment on his next check—for any reason at all. Tell him you've had a computer foul-up, or an accounting anomaly. Tell him anything; just hold up on that check and see if he gets along without tapping the accounts you know about or selling anything he owns. If you can, find out where he gets his money. If he has enough to cover the checks, then you have plenty of time to worry about the validity of their signatures."

But Williams was shaking his head paternally. "You're a bright young man, Mr. Phillips, but you don't know much about running banks. If Mr. Rosetti can cover the checks and forestall a public investigation, and if an investigation by anyone else seems unlikely, then we don't care whether the checks are valid or not."

"That seems unethical," I said, "probably because it is."

"It doesn't have to be ethical," he said coldly.
"It's policy."

"Oh. That makes it all right, I guess." He looked
at me sharply, but said nothing. "I'll leave one of
my cards on the corner of your desk, in case you
want to get in touch."

"Thank you, Mr. Phillips," he said smoothly.
"We'll be sure and call you if we find out anything
of interest. But tell me: Why bring all this to me? A
bank this size has its own investigating firm on a re-
tainer; you weren't thinking of offering your services, were you?"

"No. Far from it. I have an investigation involv-
ing Benny Rosetti, and I want other things than me
to be on his mind." I stopped. "Mr. Williams, I've
agreed to respect your confidence. In exchange
there are two things I would like. The first is that
you respect my confidence and not tell anyone of
my visit or of its purpose."

He nodded curtly. "That goes without saying.
What's the other favor?"

I took the old lady's check from my pocket.
"Could you go to the teller's window with me so I
can cash this?"

He looked at it startledly, read the amount and
smiled thinly. "So your example earlier wasn't just
general grumbling."

"No, sir," I answered solemnly. "It was very spe-
cific grumbling."

He walked around his desk, clapped me on the
shoulder amiably and insincerely and went out with
me to the front counter. I headed for the same window as before; the youngster with the little beard
and the elf looks was still there.

I plunked the check down in front of him. "Shall I endorse it?"

He looked down at it and said irritably, "Now really, Mr. Phillips." Then he saw the bank president; he shut up and looked busy. I took the check back and endorsed it.

Williams merely said, "See that this man gets his money for that check."

"Certainly." He had the guts to sound injured that anyone thought he wouldn't have cashed it. Williams nodded to him and went away.

While the teller filled out the slip, I said quietly, "Does this make me exceptional?"

"I suppose." He sounded tired. "God, I can't wait to get back to my machines!"

"I guess it's hard, fella," I said. "Believe me, if I were the bank president, you'd never see a customer face to face again."

He looked pleased, then suspicious. He handed me my dollar and receipt. "Why would that be?"

"Policy." I wandered out to get some lunch.

WHEN I GOT BACK I sorted through my mail. Three letters for Cartley—one personal and two mail order. I sent the mail orders back marked "deceased," and set the personal aside to answer later.

Then I had two form letters from companies that offered me "quick and easy correspondence with every major detective firm in the country," both for fees that would have given me quick and easy correspondence with the Prince of Wales. I threw them both out.

The last item was addressed to me, in the delicate, spidery hand of someone well educated and elderly. I opened it and found this:

Mr. Benito Rosetti requests the company of Mr. Nathan Phillips for lunch this Tuesday, April 10, at Tommy's Table d'Hôte. Twelve o'clock. No R.S.V.P.

I looked at it. There wasn't much to learn from it, other than that Mr. Rosetti was a man of breeding and that in my case he found "respectfully requests" and "the pleasure of your company" superfluous. And that he wasn't expecting regrets—which was too bad since I had plenty of them.

I noted down the appointment on my office calendar and called Pederson. "By the way, has Rosetti ever killed anyone in a restaurant?"

"Not that I know of. Why?"

"Because tomorrow I'll either have a swanky lunch, or I'll have become exceptional."

There was a moment's silence, then Pederson said, "You were going to rattle him, not get him to take you to the prom."

He hung up just as I said weakly, "I didn't ask for this." It was just as well; I probably had.

10

On Tuesday I got in my car and drove up First Avenue to Eighth Street downtown. I didn't take the freeway. Anyone who takes 35W at noon deserves what he gets, and these days too many were getting it. I parked at Washington Avenue and walked down to Tommy's Table d'hôte.

Tommy's Table d'Hôte isn't in a hotel, doesn't have fixed lunch times and certainly doesn't have fixed prices; its first owner must have liked the sound of the name far more than he did the sense. At Tommy's you don't expect to eat lunch for under thirty dollars. Three kinds of people go there: those who are rich and want everyone to know it; those who aren't rich and don't want anyone to know it; and thugs. I was a fourth kind, a guest of the third kind.

The restaurant's outside looked like somebody's house, except that the white walls were too white, the trim was too purple, and there was a fountain by the door. I tipped my stocking cap to the naked bronze lady shivering over the empty pool and went in.

The entry had a carpet so burgundy colored it made me tipsy—that and lights so dim I had to feel my way while my eyes adjusted. I didn't dare touch the walls, though; a waiter would come along and scold me for getting the flocked wallpaper dirty.

A waiter did come along, in ill-fitting full evening

dress even though it was noon. "Yes?" He did a once-over of my clothes and looked scornful. I scanned him back, but probably I only looked confused; he seemed vaguely familiar.

"I'm with another party," I said. "My name is Phillips, Nathan Phillips. Is Mr. Benny Rosetti here yet?"

Suddenly he had as much respect as three courtiers and a lobbyist. "Right this way, sir. Mr. Rosetti is already seated. I'll bring you a menu immediately, sir."

He cringed, and his jacket fit worse than ever. I put out an arm and stopped him as he was moving away; he turned and stared anxiously into my face. It was too dark to see him well, but he was at least five years younger than I was. He said uneasily, "Is anything wrong, sir?"

"Stop worrying. I never shoot people in restaurants. I'm seeing Mr. Rosetti on business—his business, not mine. I'm as scared as you are."

I patted his shoulder; then for kicks I patted his breast pocket. Any harder and I'd have hurt my knuckles. "Well, well, remind me to tip *you*. Do all the waiters in this place double as gunmen?"

The scared-but-smooth pose disappeared; he glared at me. "Don't worry about the others. It only takes one for you."

"Forget it. Go shoot someone out of a chair so I can sit down."

"This way," he snarled.

I sighed. "To think only yesterday he called me 'sir.'"

He led me almost all the way to a table where an older man was seated alone. As the waiter turned, I put my arm through his, clamping down, and stood on his foot.

"Mr. Rosetti," I said softly. The old man looked

up. "I would like to introduce you to a man who is not a waiter. He carries a gun, and he's no friend of mine. Is he a friend of yours?" I let go of him. He knew Rosetti was watching him; he wasn't going anywhere.

Rosetti looked him up and down, slowly and carefully. "No," he said. His voice was gentle and sad, like the voice of an old man who does nothing but raise gardenias and tropical fish. "I certainly didn't ask him to watch you. No, he's no friend of mine. Once he was, perhaps, but I'm afraid now he never will be again." He smiled.

The man in the dinner jacket paled.

"You can go now," I said. The man didn't move, just looked at Rosetti. Rosetti nodded. The gunman spun around with obvious relief and vanished.

I turned to Rosetti. "With all due respect, what have you got that I haven't got?"

He smiled. "Sit down." I sat down. A waiter appeared from nowhere. "Do you mind if I order for you, young man?" Rosetti asked, then said to the waiter, "Chateaubriand, green salads and a bottle of Saint-Julien." He turned to me and asked, "How would you like your meat?"

"Medium rare," I said, more to the waiter than to him. The waiter nodded.

Rosetti regarded me with faint disapproval. "The meat is tender enough, and you won't savor it so well if it is overcooked." When I didn't change my order he sighed and said, "Very well. Mine as usual." The waiter nodded again, almost imperceptibly. "And bring the salad right away." The waiter was gone.

Rosetti said, "I'm impressed, Mr. Phillips. How did you know to check the first waiter for a gun?"

I sipped at my glass. Rosetti, not surprisingly, had ordered me a Scotch and water, no ice. "It's not a big thing. I just get dubious when a kid waiter in a place this good wears a badly fitting jacket and stares at me long and hard to make sure he'll know me again. You can buy your way into any job in this town.''

Rosetti put his own drink down and toyed with a breadstick. ''Quite right. It was careful of you to worry about such small things.''

''I try to be careful about gunmen.'' A grinning man in a white hat and apron brought out the salad and began tossing it quickly and expertly on a tray beside the table. Croutons flew like hail, and not a one missed the bowl.

Rosetti said solemnly, ''It is good to be careful. I hate to talk business at lunch, but if you are not careful these next few days, you need never worry about gunmen again.'' He picked up his fork and began sorting delicately, gracefully, through the lettuce.

He saw that my hand was still at my side and said irritably, ''Oh, take your hand away from your gun and enjoy the meal. I wouldn't shoot anyone at lunch, and no one else would shoot you while I was at the table.''

''I'll believe that last part, sir.'' I picked up my fork. He raised his eyebrows but made no response.

We ate quietly for a few minutes. That was good. We had little to talk about, and it had to last a meal. The salad was perfect. When you get good lettuce in Minneapolis in April, you know you're eating rich. I felt like I was chewing dollar bills.

As the meat arrived, Rosetti said, ''You're not a person for small talk, are you?''

''I won't talk shop with you, and you don't want to hear my life story. What could we possibly talk about?''

''There's no need to be rude.''

"I'm sorry," I said, and I really was. "I guess you make me nervous."

He smiled sympathetically at me. "I hoped I would, you know. It's a much better way of doing business." He took a forkful of potatoes, and I noticed his hand shook slightly. His other hand wandered on the tablecloth.

"It's not nice to scare people," I said, just for filler.

"Oh," he replied, "but it's so much nicer than other things I might do." His fingers on his free hand began fluttering rapidly on the table, and he toyed for a moment with his potatoes.

Suddenly he stood up. "Excuse me," he said, his suaveness returning. "Go ahead and eat in my absence. I won't be gone long."

While he was gone I ate the rest of the meat. Maybe he was right about the flavor, but I wouldn't have wanted it as rare as his, almost red on the outside. He was right about the tenderness; I could cut it with my fork.

I thought about Rosetti's remark about not being shot while he was at the table. I raised my napkin to my lips, slipped my gun from my shoulder holster, slid the napkin back down to my lap and held the gun there in my left hand. I tried to eat methodically but not hurriedly; it was hard to keep from speeding up. I wanted to have lunch mostly done when he came back.

I was all but finished when he returned, wiping his nose and walking with a springy, almost a jaunty step. His eyes had been bright before; now they practically sparkled. He glanced quickly but cautiously down at my plate and said, "My, but you made short work of that. You must learn to relax at mealtime."

While I slipped the gun into my front pocket I ate another forkful of mashed potatoes. It wasn't just to hide the movement; they were the smoothest potatoes I'd ever had. Someone had put a lot of enthusiasm into beating them. I answered after I swallowed, "Not all of us find it as easy to relax as you do."

That made no impression. He looked at me alertly, then picked up his knife and fork and began slicing his steak. "I suppose we should get down to business—my business. Were you hired to find Steven Grey?"

"I'm not saying that's what I was hired for, but I am looking for him." I stared, fascinated. Rosetti was slicing with the deftness of a surgeon, making quick, neat, sharp-edged rectangles out of the meat. I couldn't have done better with a razor blade and a straightedge.

He set down his knife and fork abruptly and looked at me coldly. "Don't." He took his handkerchief out, turned his head and sniffed once more, then folded the handkerchief neatly and put it back in his breast pocket.

I did my best to look hurt. "That's it? Just 'don't'? Not even a small money offer?"

He picked up his fork again. "Believe me, if it weren't for the bad precedent, I would buy you—and at my price, you would accept."

I leered. He frowned, and said, "Stop trying to look coy. It makes me ill." I went back to looking hurt. He went on, "But if I bought you, cheap as you would be, there would soon be other people to buy. Many of them wouldn't be as cheap as you are."

"There aren't many that are. If you're not eating your steak, could I have the doggie bag?"

He looked at his plate, at the meat cut out in completely uniform pieces. The inside of the steak was nearly raw; either he had been given the center slice of the piece I'd had an end of, or two separate wholes had been cooked for us. He stared intently, then shook his head and said to himself, "No. Not yet." He looked across at me. "I have one thing to ask you: are you still going to look for Grey?"

"I'm still planning on it."

He meticulously pronged a piece of meat dead center. "Then I'm very sorry for you, Phillips." He put it in his mouth.

"First no 'sir,' now no 'Mr.,' " I commented sadly. "Maybe it's my breath."

He wasn't listening. He put another piece of meat in his mouth, and another, and began chewing them. His jaw worked sideways, with a tearing motion, as much as it did up and down. The meat was tender, but he was tough. He gnashed it like it was still alive and struggling. He stared down at the plate and his eyes glowed. The only expression I could remember like his was one I'd seen many years ago—on a farm dog that was eating a young rabbit.

I was through eating. I signaled a waiter and got one with only two tries. When he came up, I said, "Could I have my check, please."

He didn't quite goggle. "You want separate checks?" He added, barely, "Sir."

Rosetti swallowed hastily, but still savoring the meat as it went down. "That really won't be necessary—"

"I insist." I glared at the waiter. He scuttled off, one ear cocked for the sound of gunfire. I turned back to Rosetti. "You threatened me. That means I don't want you to buy me lunch, and I wouldn't buy yours."

He dabbed at his mouth with a napkin and replied sadly, "But you're so young; I thought it was the least I could do."

I was as annoyed as I was nervous. "No, you can do less than that, and you can wait to send flowers, too. I never said I was tough, and I don't try to be—but don't waste time scaring me. I work just as well scared.''

The waiter came back with my check; I paid it—I could eat for a week on less—and tipped him five dollars. He waited for more, shrugged, thanked me and pocketed it as he left.

I got up. ''Goodbye, Mr. Rosetti.'' He wasn't paying attention; he was blissfully gnashing on little rectangles of steak. ''I enjoyed lunch with you. Would you like me to stay and scream for you while you chew on that?''

He regarded me disinterestedly and swallowed. ''We'll see each other twice more. After the third time, you won't see me.''

''Oh. Well, I'm going. Do me a favor, though: can you tell me who the waiter with the gun was working for and what he'd want with me?''

Suddenly Rosetti was alert again. ''No. I never saw him before.'' I found that hard to believe. ''He looks like a hired gunsel; who else would waste money and time acting like a waiter? Maybe he wants to kill you.'' He chuckled. That was supposed to be funny.

I chuckled back. ''Maybe he wants to do business with me. Maybe if I can find Grey, this guy will want to know about it, so he'll know what to do about you.''

He looked thoughtful. I turned and left.

When I got outside I took my gun from my hip pocket and holstered it. The fake waiter wasn't in sight, and he didn't shoot at me from a passing car. Maybe it was his lunch hour.

11

NOTHING MUCH HAPPENED that afternoon, and I needed the break. It was time I took a breather and waited to see what came of the trouble I'd stirred up.

I had a short wait; when I got home early that evening the phone rang. Marlowe cleverly ran between my legs at the first ring; I made it to the phone by the third. I picked it up too fast and bumped my lip. "Ouch. Hello?"

"Nathan Phillips?" It was a low warm voice I couldn't place. I wanted to—badly—and only partly because it had panic in it.

"Speaking. Take a deep breath and relax. Who is this?"

"Deirdre Ryan. I've got to talk to you, right away."

"Okay, right away. Same place as last time?"

"No!" My ear buzzed as she added quietly, "No, I can't go there."

"Fine. Someplace else, then; calm down. Where?" I hoped I sounded calm; I wasn't very.

"There's a little town called New Market, just off 35, south of the Cities. Take the exit to it, then turn off east instead and take the first gravel road north. I'll be parked at the first corner north."

Sounded like spy stuff. "What time?"

"Soon as you can. An hour would be way too long."

"I can get there in forty minutes. What's your hurry, you think you're being followed?"

"Mister, I know I am. I spotted the guys when I came in here. I'm calling from a booth in the Stooker's café on the highway. Two men just came in and sat down across from me; they're watching me."

"No chance they're on the make, or they just want to use the phone?" I didn't have much hope.

"Be serious, will you? I'm in big trouble. If I leave here and don't get to you in time, I've had it." She said miserably, "Honest to God, I've never had a break in my life, and I guess I never will, now."

"Don't talk like that. I'll come down and get you out of there. You can tell me what you know, and I'll put you on a bus to someplace else." I was babbling. "Maybe California—would you like California?"

"I'd like anyplace." She sounded sad and dull and far away.

"Leave the café exactly thirty minutes from now. I'll meet you at the place you named; I'll get there the same time you do. Why'd you pick that place, anyway?"

"I figured it's deserted, so it's safe."

"That's city reasoning; a crowd would be safer. Just—"

"Just be there," she said with the exasperated sharpness of the terrified. "I need you."

"No, Deirdre, wait. Stay there. Stay—" She had already hung up. I hung up, too, put out Marlowe and was on the interstate south inside of a minute and a half.

Traffic was bad for the first few miles, late-rush-hour stuff, and nothing I could do about it. I did a steady fifty, trying to slide into holes that weren't there, dodging fenders and watching for police cars. I wasn't speeding, but the way I was driving there had to be something to haul me in for. I took the bend toward Bloomington without slowing down; the traffic thinned out a little. I was up to sixty by the time I passed the mall exit, seventy as I got into the newer suburbs. I wished I'd had time to sneer at them; if they hadn't been built there wouldn't be so much fast money loose in the Cities, and I probably wouldn't have been playing with guns and gunmen. Or maybe I was kidding myself about that.

I settled down as the traffic sped up, and I thought about what I could do. There wasn't much; she'd be dead before the police could get there if I stopped to call. It was a cinch she wouldn't think to call them. If neither of us called them, I'd look pretty silly trying to take two men on alone. I hoped Deirdre didn't realize just how bad a fix she was in. I sped up, still thinking.

A state highway patrol car went by on the other side of the median. I started to slow down, then accelerated, swerving and meandering intentionally. In my rear-view mirror I could see him slowing up. I kept the pedal to the floor and lane-straddled till I was out of sight. I slowed up after that; there was no sense in reaching my exit before the patrol caught up with me.

Five miles before the New Market turnoff a patrol car showed up behind me, gaining slowly. I fish-tailed once for effect, nearly losing control in the process, then accelerated out of it. My car didn't surge ahead—cars these days never do—but I picked up speed steadily until I was doing ninety. By eighty the flashing lights were on behind me.

Even with my lead, they nearly caught up before the turnoff. I got an advantage briefly; two cars were going side by side and I swerved past them on

the right, cutting too close in front of them. The
right-hand car hit the brakes, and the cop had to
slam on his to avoid a collision.

That gave me some time; it meant I could take the
exit ramp at a mere fifty. I didn't quite skid off; my
front end was slewing around the whole time, both
fenders about a yard off opposite reflector posts. I
kept thinking I heard Cartley telling me to slow
down. God, I wanted to listen.

The gravel turnoff nearly ended it. I'm not used
to gravel anymore; it slides, and so do your wheels.
I stayed on the road, but suddenly the patrol car
was close behind me. There was a squad car of some
kind following the patrol car—probably some county sheriff, notified by the patrol too late for a road-
block.

I would just make it to the corner, with luck. They
were closing fast. Ahead I saw the taillights of a car.
If I hadn't been busy staying on the road, I'd have
slumped with relief.

Then I saw the other car, beyond it.

I pulled in behind them, fast. As I swerved I could
see people for a moment in my headlights: three figures, shadows against dirty snow, black on white.
One was holding the middle one up. The left one
had his hand raised and his shoulder pulled down
and back. The middle one should have been struggling but wasn't.

As I slowed I stuck my gun out the window and
fired in the air. I wanted the cops, barely behind
me, to pull their guns out; I wasn't in enough trouble, anyway. As I jumped out one of the men ahead
fired, still holding Deirdre upright. I ducked, stumbling off the road. It must have looked like I'd been
hit; they seemed surprised when I came up out of
the ditch, shooting as I ran.

I shot high and wide to avoid hitting Deirdre. The

two men dropped her and ran to their car, roaring off as I came even with them. They had plenty of time. I retreated to the ditch and caught Deirdre as she fell; she toppled slowly off the edge of the road like a badly hung scarecrow off a pole.

I dropped my gun and cupped her skull with all ten fingers; I bawled for the police. They were there—surrounding me with their guns out—and none of them had followed the car that left. I didn't bother holding still. "Who knows first aid here?"

They stopped, puzzled. "I do." It came from a young man with sandy-colored curly hair and the stuck-out chin of an Irish prizefighter.

"Help this girl." He nodded, leaped down and cradled her head while I ripped off my coat and spread it in the snow; we moved her gently onto it. My hands were red and damp; I wiped them in the snow.

It took him all of fifteen seconds to decide she needed an ambulance. While they called for it an older man from the sheriff's department came up, and the questions began. I started answering, but I wasn't paying much attention. I kept looking at my hands in the near darkness, wondering how clean they really were.

12

THE MAN FROM THE SHERIFF'S OFFICE was a weather-beaten veteran named De Cunha. He looked more like a farmer than a policeman; his face was lined and leathery from too much sun and wind, too little water and peace of mind. "You have explaining to do," he said coldly.

"A little."

He exploded. "Little, hell. Reckless driving, ninety in a fifty-five, ninety in a forty-five, ninety at night—the only thing we can't get you for is loitering."

"We were told he was drunk," one of the state troopers said woodenly.

De Cunha looked at him contemptuously. "Well, he ain't. Any fool can see that."

The trooper stood up ramrod straight; they must teach them all that somewhere. "The first report said he was swerving and lane-straddling." He turned and looked at me.

"That was the only way I could get your attention."

If he'd been slouching at all he would have stiffened. De Cunha smiled. The trooper said curtly, "Do you want to handle this, Deputy De Cunha?" He stressed the "deputy" and De Cunha winced; I gathered some local politics were involved.

"Being as this is a county road, yes."

"All right. We'll send you a report in case you

need help filing charges.'' He walked away like a general after troop inspection; they must teach that at the same place as standing up straight.

De Cunha watched him go. "He won't send the reports," he said conversationally. "He'd rather see me mess up on the arrest." Then he turned hard again. "This one would be hard to mess up. Now, tell me why you wanted to find a cop and why you couldn't have phoned. And you better tell it slow and careful, so I can swallow the hard parts.''

I explained in detail, only leaving out the name of my client. I put Rosetti's in twice, but De Cunha wasn't impressed; so much for name-dropping. The whole time I was standing in a sports coat in the snow; he wasn't impressed by that, either. He interrupted me twice.

The first time he was still mad. "I s'pose you can't tell me who your client is?''

"Not unless you subpoena me. If you have any excuse to, though, go ahead; I don't like my client much.''

"Mmm.'' He rasped his throat and spat. "Go on.''

The second time I was talking about Deirdre. The ambulance crew had come and were loading her up. De Cunha said, "Hold on a second," and walked up to where she lay. The ambulance crew glared at him impatiently, but waited.

The young deputy had done a good job, putting blankets on and around her without moving her head. The medic with the ambulance crew had strapped some kind of plastic cradle on her skull; it covered her head like a football helmet. The ambulance crew had tossed the blankets aside—I grabbed one—and put a thin, taut reflective plastic over her body—much warmer than blankets; wrapped around her it looked almost fashionable instead of makeshift.

De Cunha said, "Go ahead" to the crew, then searched around where she had lain, working his way up to the road. Finally he checked her car and pulled a brown leather purse with a shortened strap from the front seat. He slipped it on his shoulder, putting his arm over it. It rode between his armpit and his elbow; if he'd clamped down, dynamite couldn't have blasted the purse free. "She wasn't worried about purse thieves, was she?"

He turned it upside down and shook it over the car hood. Three kinds of eye shadow, two lip glosses and a roll of bills fell out. "She a good friend of yours?" he asked, deadpan.

"Let's just say we did business together." The young deputy snickered; De Cunha looked at him and he shut off like someone had pulled a switch. We all watched as the ambulance disappeared toward New Market.

"She'll live." We both turned to the young deputy. "She's got a fractured skull and some other breaks, but none compounded. There may be brain damage." I looked at him unbelievingly; he turned and stamped back to the car.

"He doesn't really know that," De Cunha explained. "He's a good boy, but he thinks he's smart. He's on leave from medical school, going back when he makes enough money."

"I didn't know they let people do that."

"Maybe they don't. Chances are if he's out too long, when he goes back he'll have to start over." He sighed. "He's kind of sore about it already. We give him a little leeway. It ain't just school; he's trying to support his mother. Only she has a farm she won't sell, or he wouldn't have to. Makes him bitter; that kind of thing's hard on a man."

I walked back toward my car. "He must have some good in him then, or he wouldn't bother.

What are you going to do about the traffic charges?''

He spat again. "I hate like hell to do this, especially when you probably planned it this way—but if those state boys don't come through on their report, worst I can do is ticket you for ten over the speed limit on gravel."

"You could always say sixteen."

He looked at me, and his lips moved for a second. "Sixteen, right. Hell with them kilometers, though—I ain't using them till somebody makes me." He opened his car door. "Anyway, what I figure is this. I'll check you out with the Minneapolis police and just give you a warning if you're okay. If you're pulling something fancy, or if you've done this a lot, I guess I'll have to swallow my pride and call the state boys for their report." He glared. "And then I'll nail your ass for making me get outside help in an election year. Sheriff'll say it was my fault."

Lights went on in my head. "You're running for sheriff?"

"This fall. I was sheriff for twelve years before the last election. Now I patrol around New Market, and one of my old deputies is sheriff. A good boy, but it's embarrassing for a man my age. By the way, the patrol and I are going to be sitting up nights waiting for you to do it again." I didn't say anything. He slammed his hands on the dash. "Goddammit, son, talk back. I know I ain't scaring you."

"Maybe not, but you have to say it and I have to listen."

He chuckled. "Come on to the office. I gotta get a statement from you on those two men that beat up the young lady."

My statement wouldn't do much good; nobody had seen the men, their car or their car license plates close up. My description—and everyone else's—would come to "two very bad men."

Just before I climbed into my car De Cunha called out, "Is there somebody we should notify for the girl?"

"Not that I know of." I thought. "She might have insurance, and they might pay off, but I doubt it on both counts. I'll check around in the city, see if she has any friends."

"That'd be nice of you. She ought to have friends."

"Why?"

"To balance things off. She has had enemies."

Suddenly I felt tired and much older than De Cunha. I stared at the bleached-out road lit by his headlights. "No. I had enemies. They just spilled over, that's all."

He gave me a cold stare. "Then you were right about one thing."

"What's that?"

"When you didn't say you were her friend."

All the way to the sheriff's office I tried to argue with that to myself. I didn't do too well.

13

WHEN I GOT BACK to Minneapolis, there was nothing to do but sleep. I couldn't, though; I had too much on my mind. So I sat up annoying Marlowe and fidgeting slowly until four in the morning. I didn't solve a thing, but at least I got so I could get in bed with myself and not despise the company.

In the morning I had a cup of tea, scratched Marlowe's stomach for luck—he scratched back for his luck—and went out to do some pavement pounding. First I left a note on my office door in case Greasy should drop by, telling him to go into the outer room and wait. Then I went out looking for him.

He wasn't hard to find. The taco stand in downtown Minneapolis is a good cheap breakfast for a bad cheap man. I waded in through the smell of fried onions and Tabasco and the smell of sizzling meat substitutes, and took a look around. The counter was clean on top and covered with taco drippings on the sides. Even in April there were flies in here. The napkin holders had gum parked on the sides instead of the bottoms; the pressed-wood tables had sticky-looking blots on them and suspicious-looking gouges made with ink pens. It wasn't the kind of place to take your mother or the health inspector. Behind the counter was a yellowed sign with grease spatters on it; the sign said in felt-tip penned letters, The Management Does Not Encourage Tipping. It certainly didn't.

In the corner, freshly painted and waxed, with immaculately polished glass and scarless chrome trim, was the best-cared-for pinball machine I'd ever come across. There weren't even cigarette burns on top of it; there was an ashtray built into the wall beside it. Greasy was leaning meditatively on a table to its right, watching a fourteen-year-old black boy with enormous hands bump and juggle his way to pinball victory over an annoyed white kid in a vinyl jacket and cowboy boots. They looked like any two kids in a pool or pinball joint. Twenty dollars changed hands on that game; then they played another, double or nothing. I don't know; maybe kids these days have bigger allowances.

After the second game was over and the white kid pocketed his twenty back, Greasy looked at them as close to innocently as he'd ever managed. It missed by a mile. "Say, that looks like fun. Could I play against one of you two? We wouldn't have to bet much. . . ."

He trailed off as they both looked at him pityingly and walked out without saying a word, pausing only to thump another boy, slightly older and more heavyset, on the chest and jerk a thumb toward the door.

Greasy was still looking after their wallets regretfully when I slapped a quarter on the machine and said, "I'll play you."

He almost blew it. His ears wiggled and he started to say my name, but he thought better of it and stopped. Then he thought better still and smiled craftily. "How about putting five on it?"

I hissed between my teeth, "I don't want to, you money-grubbing weasel."

He hissed back through the gaps in his teeth, "You got to make it look real, you tightwad fool."

I slapped my five down, put the quarter in and

started. While the ball bounced around I asked conversationally, "Know any hookers in this town?"

"You kidding? I know them, but can't afford 'em; they don't seem to like me."

"Come on— A clean-cut ladies' man like you? I want you to—oops." I nearly lost the ball down a side chute.

"You got to jiggle it more. You want me to talk to them, or find you one or what?"

My first ball went down the middle. "Hell. What I want is for you to go down to Hennepin and gossip about Deirdre Ryan. Say she got beat up last night, say you bet it was those guys that have been hanging around her lately."

"You know how many guys hang around a whore in one night? Hey, watch it." The ball was bouncing off the right bumper lazily.

I caught it mostly by accident. "I have no idea. The point is, these two wouldn't be customers, but watchers."

The second ball fell through the right side. "Tough luck. These guys—they wouldn't be the same ones that got me?" He sounded awfully eager.

"I don't know," I admitted. "I think the guys you want work for Reedy Rentschler, but I'm not sure yet." I wasn't going to be sure, either, until Greasy kept his end of the bargain. "Get the description of these two, and see if they're Rentschler's thugs." I was betting they weren't.

The last ball slid down. Greasy sniffed. "Five thousand points." He moved in front of the machine, handing me his taco. "Want a bite, young fella?" I nearly dropped it. He shrugged and crossed his arms, so that his sling-bound arm could reach the flipper button; then he whapped the ball plunger with a quick right-handed wrist flip before slipping his right arm back under his left.

Over the thud of the ball and the steady ring of bells, Greasy asked, "Why would Reedy have her beat up?"

"Because she knew something about what happened to Grey."

He shifted and pushed the machine, catching the ball expertly before it went down the side, tossing it from flipper to flipper for setup shots. "Something about Reedy?"

"I don't think so."

"Then if it wasn't about him, why did he care?"

"Beats me. I'll figure that out when I find out if they were his men."

"What if he— Well, damn!" He'd lost his first ball, but he already had more points than I'd got in three.

"When we find that out," I said, tucking the five gingerly in his shirt pocket, "we work it from there."

He leaned on the machine casually with his good elbow. There was something annoying about being beaten at pinball by a man with one arm in a sling. "Another five says I beat your best game on each of the other balls."

"If I were dumb enough to take bets like that, I'd never have five bucks." I left as the cook ran out from behind the counter, swearing in Spanish, to wipe off the oily smears that Greasy—true to his name—had left on the glass and chrome of the pinball machine.

14

BUSINESS—REGULAR BUSINESS—WAS POOR. I super-
vised the moving out of Cartley's desk, which I had
finally finished cleaning out; then into my suddenly
spacious office I welcomed an elderly lady who said
a nasty man was following her and making her
afraid. She sat bolt upright in my good chair, fumbling at her very old, very black handbag and saying
the man was "dark and sad eyed, evil looking."

I asked why she hadn't gone to the police. "Because—" she admitted, pulling a Kleenex from her
purse and wiping with furtive nervousness at her
mouth, "—my son says this man has to do with a
plot the police and one of his close acquaintances
are making against him. He never says what it is but
hints at it constantly. It's all very upsetting."

"I'm sure he's worried for no reason, ma'am.
What does this man following you look like?"

She told me readily enough. "Dark, and baggily
dressed. He forgets he's hiding from me and he
whistles—mostly opera tunes, I think. And he turns
his right foot out when he walks."

I laughed. "With a memory and eyes and ears like
that, what do you need me for? But I know who
your man is. He's a private detective named Hal
Marino; he's not even faintly dangerous. Why don't
you ask your son where this tail came from? Frankly, he may know something about it, if you don't
mind my implication."

She relievedly shook her head. "If Bernard thinks I need watching, why, maybe I do. I wouldn't want to upset him. He's a good boy," she said confidingly, "but he has ideas, you know. No, that's quite all right; I'll just put up with being followed."

"Fine. Your choice—but don't go anywhere you wouldn't want to be caught."

She thought, then smiled. I swear she had a five-year-old's mischief in her smile. "Do you suppose he'd enjoy following me through the Institute of Arts? I've been wanting to go there, but I wouldn't want him to be bored."

I said that would be nice and suggested that if he looked bored, she could always try to ditch him. That sort of thing adds life to an otherwise dull day. I tried to refuse payment, but she insisted on giving me five dollars. She smiled again and made a little finger wave as she left. A lot of this business leaves me wondering what happens after clients leave. At least this time most of the wondering was pleasant.

The rest of the afternoon I typed a report for Mrs. Grey. I included my itemized expense account, enjoying making it up almost as much as I'd enjoyed refusing payment earlier in the afternoon. I hoped the expense account was a more successful argument. I put it and the report in the mail on the way home.

Back home I settled in to balancing my checkbook and looking over old office bills for delinquent clients. I had a lot more fees outstanding than I did checks; making checks good is a lot easier than making clients good. Both jobs were patience-and-headache work; I had not enough of the first and too much of the second. Worse, I'd run out of aspirin; I was cranky when the phone rang. I hoped it was Dave or Bernie, and almost wished I'd called them first.

The voice was loud, cocky and oddly familiar. "Phillips? This is Arnie." That was supposed to explain everything.

"I'm happy for you. Who the hell is Arnie?"

"A guy that wants to talk to you about Stiff Grey and about looking for him, on account of you ain't gonna find him."

"I like the way you talk. Are they still showing Cagney movies on TV?"

"Shut up. I don't like the way you talk, and I like to shut people up. I saw a girl shut up just the other night."

My knuckles cracked on the phone receiver. "What's your last name?"

"I better not tell you; I'm scared of trouble." He didn't sound scared.

"Is it Rumpelstiltskin?"

"What?"

"Bozo?"

"Hey now—"

"How about Rentschler?" There was no answer. "Welcome back, Arnie. Your brother Dwight home, too?"

"You talk too much to the wrong people, Phillips."

"This time I was talking to myself, and your name came up once too often. You want to talk, huh?"

"Yeah." He added slowly, "And leave Dwight out of this. He ain't working with me these days."

"Tsk, Arnie. You're not a very close family, are you?" No reply. "Tell you what: why don't you come by my apartment at seven and I'll be here."

"So will I." He hung up. Now all I had to do was wait until Greasy came back and told me where Dwight was. If he found Dwight. If he remembered to tell me, or bothered.

In the meantime I called Reedy Rentschler and

left a message. "One of your boys is working free-
lance; the other one—Dwight—is probably working
for Rosetti until something better comes along.
Want a family reunion?"

Mrs. Rentschler took the message grudgingly.
"Why bother with those two?"

"What a thing for a mother to say."

"Don't give me that. I'm their stepmother; anybody with half an eye can tell that."

"Sorry. I've missed your girlish charm lately."

"I've missed you, too. Come back within pistol
range." She hung up and I sat for a moment, thinking about the whole mess.

That only made my head worse. I pulled on my
stocking cap, but hesitated before leaving and put a
table lamp on so it was visible from the front room.
If you're expecting rough company, it's nice to
have a light on when you come home.

Once outside I was as restless as I was headachy.
I'd been hungry, for no reason I could think of, ever
since talking to Arnie. I went downtown and had a
quick dinner at a café on Nicollet. There was an all-
night pharmacy just around the corner; I made up
excuses for not walking into it until six-forty. By
then most of my headache was gone; it was mostly
hunger and too many problems. Maybe I needed to
call someone and get in trouble again.

Inside, the store was quiet, nearly empty. It
stayed open, I suppose, as a service to the desperate
customers late at night who stumble in seeking relief in the form of pills, cosmetics or magazines. All I
wanted was aspirin and a phone, but I suppose I
qualified.

In the back corner I finally found someone: a kid
moving listlessly from one foot to the other with a
broom in one hand and a comic book in the other.
The comic's cover showed a half-naked muscle boy

with a sword fighting something nasty with three arms. I tapped the kid on the shoulder and he jumped a foot, dropping the comic and clenching the broom handle with both fists.

I picked up the comic and handed it to him. "Easy—I come in peace. Where's the pay phone?"

He nodded embarrassedly toward the back and resumed his lifeless reading and sweeping before I had even turned away. Must be nice to have a job so dull you work at getting nervous.

I called the police station to ask about any leads on the Ryan beating; my call got transferred almost immediately to Pederson. As soon as he came on I asked, "What are you doing on this? She's still alive, isn't she?"

"Calm down. I didn't think she was your type, Nate. She's alive, and she'll stay that way, probably. But she's in a coma, and she's been moved from New Market to Minneapolis. We're keeping an eye on her; whatever she knows is important enough for someone to risk a murder charge suppressing it. Who thinks it's that important, Nate?"

"Rosetti," I said flatly. "Nobody else involved in this knew about her."

"Uh-huh. But this isn't his style; he never mixes criminal business and bloody pleasure."

I winced. "He hired it done. From a phone call I just got, I'd guess he hired Arnie and Dwight Rentschler, just to confuse things— That's right, they don't work for their dad anymore. Unfortunately, the Rentschler boys are both slug simple—so Reedy says. That's what made me think it was them in the first place. If Reedy's telling the truth, this beating was their version of day-to-day business practice."

"So?"

"What do you mean, 'so'?"

"So how do we find out for sure if they did it?"

"I'm seeing Arnie in a few minutes. He'll either tell me or kill me."

I could hear Pederson thinking. All he said was a noncommittal, "That might work."

"For whom? You sound like a high-school guidance counselor."

"You sound like you need one." He coughed. "I'll call you if I find out something; don't call me until you do." He slammed the phone down. Private detectives who ask stupid questions and give very few answers, stupid or otherwise, aren't popular even with friends on the force.

I picked up my gloves and looked around the drugstore. It was still almost empty; no one was within listening distance. There was a man at the counter buying cough drops from the kid. He—the man—looked familiar in that annoying way people you don't know sometimes look like people you do. This time I was sure he wasn't anyone I knew; I kept thinking he should either have looked younger, or older and more nervous.

I picked up a bottle of aspirin and asked the clerk to give it to me without a child-proof cap. I nodded to the cough-drop buyer as he went out. He grunted. Probably had a cold.

When I left the drugstore he was at the bus stop on Nicollet, searching his pockets. He turned to me apologetically. "Mister, I'm out of matches." He shuffled my way. "You got any?"

His voice made him less familiar, but his face still bothered me. I knew it should have been younger—or much older—and his hair grayer and shorter. I said I might have matches and reached into my trouser pocket.

He said, "Gee, thanks," and stumbled against me. Suddenly I knew who he looked like: a young Reedy Rentschler.

Of course, my best clues were the gun in my side and the hand jamming my own hand in my pocket.

"Move slowly down the street, Phillips. Act natural." When he whispered, the resemblance was even stronger.

"How natural can I act, walking down the street holding hands with a man?"

"That's up to you." He didn't let go; I didn't try to break free. We strolled away from the bus stop and around the corner to my car. "We gotta go talk. Into the car."

I got in from the passenger side. He slid in beside me without ever relaxing his grip or moving his gun an inch from my ribs.

I turned on the motor and pulled slowly away from the curb. He sat back but kept the gun on me. "Now, Phillips, take us someplace we won't be disturbed."

"Think of my reputation, Dwight."

"Shut up." He poked me with the gun; his voice was harsh. "How did you know it was me? Talk."

"Arnie talks too much, Dwight. He wanted to talk to me tonight. He said you—"

"Shut up, I said." Another poke. Actually, you *can* have it both ways if you're holding a gun. "Meeting him where?"

"My—" I coughed "—my office. I was headed there now."

"Then we ain't going there. Turn right." I turned right. "Does he know anyplace else to find you if you don't show up?"

"He called at my apartment before. I told him to call there if I was late or didn't show."

Out of the corner of my eye I could see Dwight grin nastily. "I think I'll be there to take a message." Still another poke. "Head home."

I should have told him not to throw me in the brier patch. "I can't do that, Dwight; he'll—"

That got me his usual answer with his usual gun. "Home, I said." I headed home, thinking dark thoughts about where I'd like to put that gun if I got the chance.

Halfway there I said, "You can quit poking me with that thing. If you want to fight, fight— Or do you only swing on women?"

He looked at me speculatively. "Maybe you can see in the dark better than I thought you could, Phillips. It seems like a shame for you."

"A real shame." I was mad enough not to care what I said and was doing too well with my guesses to shut up. "But my eyes weren't good enough to see your face at Tommy's."

"What?" He prodded me.

"Shove that thing in my ribs once more and I'll bite it out of your hand. You know what I'm talking about—the phony waiter at Tommy's Table d'Hôte."

Dwight sat back and laughed. I was too surprised to try for the gun. "Arnie the Waiter strikes again. Doesn't he ever get tired of trying that?" Suddenly he shut off and looked thoughtful. "He doesn't pull that unless he's cooking something up on his own, though."

"Arnie's a very independent man, Dwight. He broke with your new boss already; he was only working with you on that job the other night because it fit in with his own plans. Why the waiter suit?"

Dwight wasn't paying attention. "He thinks it's a classy disguise. I can't believe he's on his own. He thinks he can go up against—" He cut off.

"Rosetti?" I suggested softly. "Maybe Arnie's smarter than you think, Dwight. Rosetti doesn't seem to have done well by the last man he worked with—" My reward for being bright was another poke. I gave up and drove.

When I pulled up at the apartment I looked up and down First Avenue for strange cars. There was one about half a block away that could have been perfectly innocent. It probably wasn't; there were no lights on in my apartment. People who wait in your home uninvited are more likely to turn all lights off, thinking they've switched them on themselves without thinking. Mostly it doesn't matter what they think, as long as they turn out a light you've left on.

Dwight grunted and poked me in the ribs again. I could tell I'd have a dandy bruise there in the morning. We slid out the passenger side and headed across the street.

I came up the stairs one at a time, loudly. I stumbled once. It wasn't hard to fake; it was only hard to move slowly enough so the gun behind me wouldn't go off. I put one hand ahead of me on the banister, one over my head. "Sorry." Dwight didn't speak.

There was only room for one of us on the landing by my door; that was nice in some ways, rotten in others. My apartment was the second floor of a house; I could throw Dwight downstairs if I could push his gun aside. On the other hand, if I tried and couldn't, I'd have no place to go, and I'd probably go there.

Dwight reached into my pocket for me, keeping just out of the range where I could elbow his ribs. He dropped my keys into my palm and grinned when I turned to look at him.

I unlocked the door and rattled the knob clumsily. Even Dwight couldn't miss that it was a signal; it was a cinch he realized Arnie was on the other side of the door.

So we were neither of us too surprised when the knob pulled out of my hand and the door swung open. Then we got the surprise. The kid on the

other side had dirty-blond hair and a cut-up orange-
and-black high-school jacket. He grinned out at me
from around two old-style Colt .45 revolvers. "Get
in here." Then his eyes flickered to Dwight, standing amazed below the landing, and his nostrils
flared; he aimed the right-hand gun as he leaped
back through the doorway.

As he leaped, I leaped, rolling past Dwight. I was
out the front door before I was fully up to my feet,
dodging sideways as soon as I cleared the door
frame. I landed running. The back steps took only a
second. I could still hear shooting on the front
stairs. When I opened the kitchen door, Marlowe
passed me. He was fluffed up to the size of a basket-
ball; he yowled at me plaintively as he fled.

I tiptoed into the kitchen, grabbing the scotch
bottle from under the sink, and hurried into the living room. A bookcase hid me from the front door. I
looked over the bookcase carefully, then charged
the front door. The punk was leaning out of it,
shooting; I didn't hear any answering shots. When I
hit the door he was caught between door and
frame, unable to get either gun pointed at me. I
could take my time about hitting him with the bottle. I took all of two seconds.

He sagged immediately. I let up on the door and
he fell right back into my arms, just as if we'd
planned it together. I got him out of my way, then
peered down the silent staircase to see why nobody
had shot back. I saw.

I ran to the kitchen, snatched a dish towel and a
wooden spoon and ran back. Dwight was lying halfway down the stairs, holding his left arm over his
head and applying pressure above the wound with
his other hand. From the looks of the stairs, he
wasn't using nearly enough pressure. I lifted his
arm up, pulled the sopping coat sleeve off it, did the

same for the suit, then ripped the shirt sleeve off and tied the towel on between the wound and the shoulder. I put the spoon handle through the knot and twisted it around until the towel was tight enough that the wound stopped spurting.

I put Dwight's other hand on the spoon. "If you start bleeding again, twist on this till you stop. I'll be back."

I ran upstairs and dialed the police emergency number. "Send a squad car and an ambulance to 3375B First Avenue south. It's north of the 34th Street exit—"

"We know what Minneapolis looks like," the desk sergeant said. "What's your trouble?"

"A shoot-out and two gunmen—one bleeding, one unconscious." I jammed the receiver down and ran back to Dwight. "Still bleeding?"

"Yeah." He let go of the spoon; I grabbed it as it started untwisting. "You figure Arnie sent that kid to take you out?"

"That's what it looks like."

"Great. Instead, he took me. I lost." He held his arm higher. "That kid knocked out?"

"He'll come to in a little while; I ought to go tie him up."

He blinked, breathing hard. "If I could I'd crawl up and finish him off."

"In your condition? Nobody could do that; if both of us let go of your arm, you'd be dead before you got three feet."

"Why you think I quit shooting at him? I couldn't let go." His eyes wandered for a moment under his lowered, pain-wrinkled eyebrows. "Just rolled around on the staircase, holding on to my arm and dodging.... Phillips? Was he really that good?"

I looked at the wound in his arm and looked away. The .45 slug had traced a neat groove, per-

132

pendicular to the main artery and bisecting it just above the elbow joint. "I don't know." I considered. "Not him. He couldn't be that good. I've seen nurses do sloppier jobs with IV needles. Besides, he missed with all the other shots."

Dwight nodded, satisfied, and closed his eyes. I held his arm up and watched it bleed. That was the way we were when the sirens stopped, right out front.

The cops who came in were both rookies, with that dead-tired look new cops always have from moonlighting. It takes them a while to learn that being a cop with an off-hours job is more than just holding down two jobs.

They stepped over Dwight, who was telling them what to do with themselves, with each other and with their nearest and dearest. They took no notice. "Where's the other one?"

"Upstairs. I hit him on the head with a bottle a while back, but I haven't had time to tie him up."

They nodded wearily; they hadn't expected any better. They ran up unhesitatingly, the front one drawing his gun and the back one holding handcuffs out; they kicked the door open and were gone. Dwight glanced up as they dove into the apartment. "Guy could get killed doing that. For dirt wages." He snorted. "Crazy fools."

The stretcher crew came up the stairs almost at the dead run. "Scrap drive," the front carrier said, deadpan.

Rentschler squawked and pulled his gun out from under him with his good arm. I hadn't even thought to frisk him.

"Touch me and I'll blow your ass off."

The front man brushed past him, barely slowing down. "We just took the 35W curve at sixty, slid around two trucks to get the exit and ran two stoplights. You think you can scare us with a mere gun?" He slapped the gun aside and knelt by the wounded arm.

His partner at the stretcher's other end, following by necessity, said miserably, "I hate this. Drive up here like a maniac, then I gotta follow you around and try not to get shot. Why don't you just kill me and get it over with?"

"I keep asking myself." The front man was undoing the dish towel from Dwight's arm. "Whose macramé, here? Nice job—if you were just trying to keep him warm."

"What did you expect? I'm an amateur, not a paramedic. I didn't know there were two-man ambulance crews in the city; don't you have a third man?"

"Died on the last job." The front man undid the towel, produced an elastic band from nowhere and tied off the arm almost as the dish towel came loose. "A terrified thug with an infected hangnail shot him."

"Don't let him kid you," the back man said. "Our third man, Vince, got a broken arm when he fell on the stairs at the last place. We weren't gonna go out alone, just the two of us like this, but it's a busy night." He shivered. "Lot of accidents tonight."

"You don't seem to like your work much," I commented. "Why don't you quit?"

He picked up his end of the stretcher as his partner flipped Dwight onto it gently and effortlessly. "What, and leave show business?" All his nervousness was gone. At his signal the former front man squatted, picked up the end, and they carried Dwight downstairs, keeping him level.

The new back man said nervously, "Hey, watch it— I can barely keep up."

"Besides," the front man said, ignoring him, "if I

keep this job, sooner or later I'm bound to have a
work-related accident. And then—" he finished triumphantly as they went out the front door "—I'll
want an ambulance crew there."

From the street we could hear one voice wail, "I
hate this!" and the other say, "Cheer up, you're the
best damn straight man I ever had." I looked dazed-
ly at one of the cops, and he looked at me.

He took off his cap and said, scratching at his red
hair, "Real comics, those two. Hope you don't feel
as funny; we have some questions."

They had tough ones. I explained how I got two
gunmen to shoot at each other instead of at me;
they didn't laugh. If they hadn't been busy with the
punk, I would have been in a lot of trouble right
away.

The punk helped me out, though. As soon as he
saw me he jumped up, handcuffs and all, and
swung at me two-handed. I stepped aside and one
of the cops grabbed him. "Okay, you're wide
awake. Now for some questions." The red-haired
cop told me to stay put and headed for the kitchen.
I yelled to him where the coffee was and asked him
for a cup of tea. He didn't seem to hear me either
time.

The black-haired cop read the kid his rights slowly
and carefully, like a tired actor at a bad read-
through. The kid mimicked him all the way through;
you could tell he'd heard it before. "Now, what's
your name, son?"

"Jonathan Olav Luther Christoph Swenumson,"
the kid said sullenly. In any other city in any other
state the cop would have slugged him. This was
Minneapolis, Minnesota; the cop didn't even have
to ask how to spell it.

"Now, what are you doing here?" No answer.
"What were you doing here?" An answer, not a

constructive one. The cop doing the questioning asked the red-haired one as he came back in, "Tom, do you think he could have been? Check the bedroom."

Tom yawned. "No. No women here—no men except for the two we met on the stairs—and, in his case, no nine-year-old girls." Swenumson's eyes flashed, but he went back to being sullen. None of the usual tricks, standard since the passing of the backhand and the rubber hose, would work on this boy.

Tom looked at me. "If that's all we get from him, maybe Erno and I should work on you. You said this kid shot someone who brought you here at gunpoint?"

I glanced at Swenumson meaningfully and said, "I'll give you the whole story at the station. I had an appointment here—not with the kid—and the man on the stairs had pulled a gun on me downtown, so I led him right back here. It's shameful, what happens in downtown Minneapolis these days—"

"Sure, sure, there ought to be a law." Erno was too tired for humor. "But the kid was here to bail you out—or did he owe you a favor?"

It was funny to hear us calling him "the kid" when not one of us was over thirty-three at the outside. "Maybe he was sent here by his boss, if he was hired by Rentschler." He was young, but tough; he didn't even blink at the name.

Tom came in on cue. "Come on. Reedy Rentschler wouldn't touch a third-rate comic-book act like this one."

"I don't mean Reedy; I was thinking maybe Reedy's son Dwight that the kid shot on the stairs. Maybe it was a double cross." I didn't think that for a minute, but if he'd been hired by Arnie, the kid wouldn't be too happy at having shot his boss's brother.

The kid wasn't as good this time. His face was sullen, but his eyes looked worried and stayed that way.

"How about that," Erno said. He'd been watching Swenumson. "Kid, you shot a tough thug, a big dealer's son and a gunman's brother, all at once. Aren't you proud?" The kid looked at him but didn't say anything. "Okay, on your feet. Phillips, you can finish at the station."

As Swenumson stood up, Tom was thinking hard. He'd missed the reaction to Dwight's name. On an obvious hunch he asked quickly and sharply, "Did Phillips hire you, Swenumson?"

The question took him by surprise, as it was supposed to. Nothing else that was supposed to happen did. Swenumson stared, his eyes opened wide, and his mouth dropped. Then his eyes shut and his mouth tried to, and he started to giggle—not a tough laugh but a kid's happy, unstoppable giggle. He broke into a full laugh and tears leaked out of his eyes. He had to lean on the bookcase to keep from falling down.

"You could just have said 'no.'" Tom's face was red.

Erno said flatly, "That a new way to grill people, Tom? Crack them up till they confess?"

"Shut up." It could have been meant for his partner, or Swenumson, or me before I said anything. We all cut off, but Swenumson couldn't stop smiling.

That's the way we were when we showed up at the station: three sullen men with tired faces and no sense of humor, and one eighteen-year-old with handcuffs on and a grin he couldn't chase away.

15

PEDERSON CAME BACK to my apartment with me from the station, ostensibly for a cup of coffee. At the front door I checked my mailbox like I couldn't when I was with Dwight Rentschler. To my surprise there was a note in it. It was typewritten on a portable machine with elite type and was on green gold stationery with a picture of heather in the upper right-hand corner. It said:

Mr. Phillips:
   It has come to my attention that there was a brief indulgence in civilian gunfire upon your staircase this afternoon, and that you precipitated the quarrel. I regret to inform you that as of next week your rent will be raised an additional five dollars per month, and your damage deposit used to cover repairs to the staircase. I do not expect a recurrence of this sort of activity.

                                        Agatha Timmons

I showed the note to Pederson. He remarked, "You have to face your landlady's temper now, do you?"

"Actually, I'd call it wrath. We better get that coffee; suddenly I need it."

"Better make it tea. We've both had enough coffee downtown, and I don't want a drink just yet."

When I came back from setting the kettle on and mixing two drinks, he had Marlowe on his lap and was stroking him. Marlowe was stretched out flat, purring blissfully. "He's worse than you," Pederson complained. "I ask you where you've been, you wise off; I ask him, he purrs. Tight-mouthed pair, aren't you?"

"Except when we're eating. Here's your drink."

"I said I didn't want one just yet."

"That was a while ago."

"You're right, damn you." We sat and sipped a while, quietly. I made tea when the kettle boiled; whiskey and tea mix well and peacefully.

So, for the time being, did Pederson and I. He wanted to stay with small talk. "Do you hear from Roy's wife?"

"Oh, sure. She wrote a couple days ago, said she was glad to be back with her family and when could I come visit. Her sister never married, you know; now they're both back at home with their mother."

"Edith's mother? Say, she must be getting on by now."

I poured his tea. "She's in her eighties, I guess, and happy as hell that her family is home again."

"The old girl used to come up and visit Roy and Edith; she'd fly all the way up from St. Louis in the dead of winter and never say peep about all the snow. They started going down, instead, these past few years. Edith and her mother are pretty close."

There was an uncomfortable silence. The small talk was gone already. There had to be more of it than that.

Pederson picked up his teacup. "You called Rentschler?" I nodded. "What did he say?"

"Same as Arnie. Said he wanted to talk. He sounded upset, though."

"And you're going to see him alone?" He shook

his head. "Haven't you had enough trouble for one night?"

I said carefully, "I'm sure it'll be all right. But you didn't come over to hear about my plans; you could have asked about those at the station."

Pederson stared into his tea. "You're right. I could have." A long pause. "I didn't—yet." He looked at me apologetically and started in. "You know, Cartley and I were very good friends, as friends go." He waited for me to say something.

"He always spoke highly of you."

He looked even more uncomfortable. "Sure, sure. The point is, it isn't easy for a cop to get along with a private eye. We were bound to have our differences, but we didn't have many. Ever wonder how we managed to get along?

"I'll tell you. We got along because I knew I could trust Roy Cartley. I never worried about his doing anything illegal—never even thought about it. Of course, I knew he had plenty of opportunity; maybe once or so he might even have had the inclination. Maybe he didn't always follow the letter of the law, but what the hell— Who can? The, uh, the point is—" he looked all but miserable "—he never did anything that could get him in trouble."

"Or at least he never looked like it." I felt sullen, about twelve years old and caught red-handed at something.

"All right, he never looked like it," Pederson answered patiently. He didn't want to get mad just yet. "That means a lot to a cop. Especially to a cop who wanted to be his friend; I didn't have to check up on him and raise hell. And you know he didn't take bribes, or blackmail jobs, or anything like them or worse. All right," he said quickly as I opened my mouth. "He could get cocky about not telling the police what was going on till he wrapped up a job. I

knew that. There was a murder or two he might
have known about earlier than he admitted.''

"That's the first time I've seen a homicide cop
wave his hand airily about a murder or two. What's
a hidden stiff between friends?''

"Okay, I'll be blunt, Nate. He never looked like
he was in trouble he couldn't handle. You do. If it
got too hot for him, or he was headed for something
he knew would land him in jail, he called. You
don't. The way he played it, he never got killed or
jailed or even lost his license. You might—any of
those three.''

"Or any combination of two.''

Pederson wasn't impressed. He took a gulp of tea
and looked studiously at the fur on Marlowe's free-
swinging tail. Marlowe was getting restless; he
could feel the tension in the air.

I answered seriously, but I was slow about it.
"I'm not running against the law, and I'm not running scared yet, either. I can't make it alone,
always, and I know that—but I don't need police
help just yet. You say Roy always called. Well, he
did, but he didn't use you as a crutch when things
got tough, either. I'll call you just before I get into
something I can't get out of, and I'll call just before
I get into something illegal—but I won't call until
then. All right?''

He set Marlowe carefully on the floor and stood
up before Marlowe could just as carefully jump
back in his lap. "All right—but I hope you shouldn't
have called earlier tonight.''

I hoped so, too. "I did call earlier tonight; you
were mad as hell.''

"Don't be cute. You called to get information, not
help. You've been treating the cops like a public
library. You've been treating me like the reference
desk.'' He looked worried and sorrowful and pity-

ing all at once. "What the hell, that was how you wanted it—but it makes me sick. We could have been friends." He shoved his chair in. "Call when you need help." He stuck his right arm into his coat and struggled with the left.

I hopped up. "Thanks for being concerned." He ignored that. I helped him into his left sleeve; he ignored that, too.

He turned in the doorway at the top of the stairs. "One last thing, Nate. If you want to get out of the business, all you have to do is give me the word. I could get you a job on the force— Hell, with a little luck I could get you a job investigating for the D.A.'s office."

"Thanks for the offer, but I worked for the D.A.'s office some, remember? D.A.'s have a nasty habit of giving up for political reasons, among others unrelated to law. And as for being a cop, you know how bad I'd be at taking orders."

He didn't look worried at all anymore, just cold and hard and ready to put the cuffs on somebody. "Orders? Phillips, you're not even good at taking advice." He turned and walked downstairs, not too slowly.

I went back in and picked up the teacups and whiskey glasses, taking them to the kitchen. Marlowe rubbed against me affectionately and looked meaningfully at the counter cupboard. He must have felt hungry. I felt like hell.

16

THERE WERE THICK WHITE CLOUDS driving across the moon when I drove up to the Rentschler house. It was on a corner—a big, dark, square, close-to-empty place with one light burning.

Mrs. Rentschler met me at the door, at home as in the office. "Thank you for coming," she said quietly. "He's been waiting." She added with more of her old style, "If it wouldn't break his heart I'd nail those two brats myself for this."

I said it was a good idea, then edged beyond her and down a lightless hall to a well-lit room. Reedy was there leaning over a huge dining-room table with two unused place settings on it.

He turned as I came in. "Phillips." Even compared to his normal voice it was hoarse. He was grayer, and his collar was wrinkled where he'd tried to loosen it after it was already unbuttoned. "Dwight—"

"Dwight is okay. They gave him two pints of blood, and they're keeping him in the hospital till he's well enough to go to jail. Before they took him in he told two cops what to do and where to go, and he pulled a gun on the stretcher boys. Before I left the hospital I told him I'd see you; he didn't have any message." Dwight did have a message, but it wasn't the kind to give a man I wanted information from. Certainly not a worried old man with family troubles and a broken throat.

"Thanks. Thank you. I couldn't go." He looked haggard. The edges of his lips were talcum white from antacid tablets. "If the cops thought I was in on this, they'd wrap around me like a wet sheet and I'd have to close down for a month."

He patted my shoulder, then pulled his hand back. "How come you bothered?" he whispered. "What was in it for you?"

"Information." No use being subtle. "You didn't testify much at Grey's trial, and your testimony made the jury think Grey hadn't done it. You and the other big shots in the Twin Cities knew all about that murder, but after the testimony I'd swear you were all amnesiacs. Because of you, I ended up searching through twenty bars, thirty diners and any number of pool halls for witnesses that couldn't have existed."

"Who says—"

"They couldn't have existed. We were looking for men who saw a gunman leave the scene of a crime, still shooting. They would have remembered. We would have found them, if they'd existed; we were that thorough. The D.A. thought it was silly even to try, but he had to check. Now it doesn't matter anymore and it'd be your word against mine if I decided to set you up for a perjury trial. What really happened the day Grey killed Grogan? And don't say he didn't, and don't say 'who says.'"

Reedy picked up another antacid tablet and chewed on it thoughtfully. "I can tell you that. You're right, it doesn't matter anymore; and if I got hauled in I could deny it all.

"We were in a big meeting upstairs at the Mc-Neary—you know that dumpy-looking place downtown?"

"I know it, but it's called the Villomar now; it

changes names and owners at least once a year. Why would you meet in a slum like that?"

"Ed Grogan owned it; it seemed like a good place to meet. We didn't want too much publicity, you know?"

"You got more than you wanted. Go on."

"Anyway, there we were: me, Irish Ed Grogan, Grey and a couple penny-ante operators—guys like Barberi, Burnout Jensen and the kid we called Bright Eyes. Those last two were what you call your average fried minds, leftovers from when kids took acid, but we invited them to meetings, anyway—just to keep track of them.

"We knew it was going to be tense. All of us wanted to know who Grey thought he was, moving in on our—" he looked uncomfortable "—customers. And before that, there was his run-in with Dumont. Nobody ever proved he'd killed Dumont, but all of us knew it; he kept bringing it up without ever admitting it. You know how that goes in this business." He started pacing back and forth in front of the table, talking more to himself than to me.

"I said Grey was moving in on established markets and that he could either buy in or stop it. I didn't threaten him; I just wanted a business deal." He looked over to see if I believed him. I nodded. "Grey laughed at me." His whisper was venomous but wondering. "Laughed—at one of the biggest operators in the Cities.

"I figured, fine, if he works that way he'll be out of business in a year one way or another. Me, I can wait—that's how I stayed in the business so long. Not that I'd wait forever, understand."

He fixed an eye on me to make sure I understood. I didn't nod this time. He scowled and went on irritably. "Anyway, Irish Ed jumped up and said, 'You try and work in my market, you'll die young.'

"Grey just looked at him with a dead, blue white stare—that stare was why they called him Stiff, you know—and said he didn't see Grogan's name sewn into any buyer's shirts.

"Once Ed got his Irish up, he couldn't stop for love or money. So he told Grey, 'You're a half-smart college punk that's too young to know better'— Grey was over thirty, but he still looked that young—and after that he said, 'You don't know what it's like yet to get beaten or shot, and maybe it's time you learned.' He said he might teach Grey whether Grey went along with us or not. Ed wasn't blood simple or anything, but when he got mad he'd talk wilder than anyone I ever knew, all kinds of threats and rough promises. When he was calm again he'd just grin and say his temper was a business asset. All those Irish are like that."

I had a coughing attack; listening to that dry throat was killing my own. Rentschler pounded me on the back, then took out a box of throat lozenges and gave me one. He took two himself.

"You all right? Good. Anyway, I was trying to calm Ed down, and Burnout and Bright Eyes were laughing like happy idiots, while Barberi sat back and tried to figure out who he'd be best off siding with. I saw pretty quick the meeting was going nowhere, so I said let's call it off unless somebody besides me or Irish had something to say to Stiff the Snow Man.

"Nobody did, and we all stood up to leave, when Grey said, 'I have something to say.' He did it in that flat, calm, don't-give-a-damn voice that makes you want to duck. Anyway, he says, 'You've each been trying to scare me in your own ways. How can I convince you that I don't scare?' "

Rentschler stopped talking and stared out the window. For a moment the moon was free of clouds, and the dirty snow piled by the curb and the sidewalk looked milky and immaculate. "God," he said hoarsely. "Now I got the time to look out once in a while, there's nothing to see."

He shook his head. "So, Grogan was full up to his ears with this don't-scare talk. He shook free of my arm, where I'd started leading him away, and yelled, 'I don't scare at all. And I don't make threats, just promises, and a promise to you is one I'd love to keep.' He stood with one hand on his hip and one in his pocket and laughed at Grey. He said, 'If you knew about fights instead of books, maybe you wouldn't be the stupid failure you're going to be, you poor bastard.'

"Then Grey relaxed and said, 'Then I can convince all of you, easily, that I will never scare.' He said it just like that—only not in a whisper—and his gun seemed to come out of nowhere. Ed roared and pulled out his gun. Grey fired four times into Ed, not really aiming for anything—at least that's the way it looked.

"I guess he was a better shot than he wanted to be; Ed kept his gun coming up but dropped it on the table before he could shoot. A couple of us wanted to hold him up, but Grey waved his gun and said, 'Stay back.' We didn't argue with him; by now Grey didn't care who was hurt or what came of it."

Rentschler's voice was soft now, even for him. It rustled sadly, like dry branches in the wind. "Ed pulled himself up by a table leg, after he'd gone down, and reached for the gun. He picked it up three times, but it was heavier every time. The last time he was leaning on both elbows, trying to hold it steady, panting and gasping like an old man carrying a bag of cement upstairs. He got a finger around the trigger. Grey just watched him—didn't try to stop him at all. Irish was covered with sweat, peering along the sight at Grey.

"Then he fell onto the tabletop and slid off, still holding the gun. I think he was dead before he hit the floor. None of us moved but Grey; he tried to take Grogan's pulse, only there wasn't one. He got back up and stared around the room for half a minute like he'd lost something. Then he whirled and shot out a window, walked over and beat the rest of the glass out with his left hand while he kept his gun on us. He got a bad cut, but didn't seem to care.

"He wiped his left hand on his trousers without looking and said slow and hard, for us to remember, 'A man shot Grogan from the window. I'm going out after him.' He hopped on the fire escape, and we heard some shots. He ran down, and we heard some more in the alley." He stopped and looked at me in silence. It took me a minute to realize that was the end of the story.

I nodded, not saying anything. What he'd told fit everything I remembered from the trial investigation—Grey's quiet insistence on an unknown killer, his scarred left hand, the gun with all six chambers empty, found in an alley and untraceable, and the shots heard in the street. The untraceable gun, a pawn-shop relic, was the one that had shot Grogan.

"So you were all scared of Grey?" I said, just to say something. "I can't buy that. What happened?"

Reedy swore at me bitterly—a vicious sound like an angry cat in pain. "You ought to know what. We all figured then that Grey'd really trapped himself; we were ready to sing like the Mormon Tabernacle Choir. It was because of us he got arrested; we said he was the only one of us that had a gun there. But we didn't come forward and testify yet. We figured there was enough to arrest him on, and we didn't want to talk too much till he was on trial and we

were on the stand. Why take chances early when
he'll be out on bail, right?''

I didn't say anything. He glared and said for me,
''Right. So it was maybe thirty-six hours after the
shooting they arrested him. We figured we'd keep
our mouths shut, in public at least, right up to the
day of the trial.

''The day we were going to start choir rehearsals,
I got a call from Burnout saying he'd got a note that
looked like a threat, and who the hell was Benny
Rosetti?''

''He was in your business, and didn't know who
Benny Rosetti was?''

Rentschler looked pained. ''He got into it as an
amateur, a college kid who made extra money. Even
with the volume of business he did, he and Bright
Eyes were both still amateurs.'' He shrugged. ''I got
my own letter an hour later. It said, 'It would be bad
policy to say anything you are not totally sure of at
the trial of Mr. Steven Grey. His new partner, Mr.
Benito Rosetti, urges your cooperation with the law
so that Grey's import business, now undergoing ex-
pansion, may see him back as soon as possible.' I
never saw such a formal goddamn threat, you
know?''

''I've talked to Rosetti. The man is a formal
threat.''

Rentschler said, ''That's the truth. So the rest of us
got together without Grey that night. Burnout and
Bright Eyes left town by midnight. I was glad to see
them go even when some hard boy from Chicago
moved in on most of their business, and Grey and Rosetti got the rest. It got rid of the two craziest witnesses and made everyone think Grey had bought
their absence.''

I remember how Cartley and I and a few other
hired hands had combed the Twin Cities to find the

two men Reedy had named. Bright Eyes's real name was Schwarzenfagg; he was lucky to have a nickname handy. Burnout and he never surfaced again. "Their absence made it a lot easier for Grey at the trial. Thanks; it's nice to know, finally, what really happened."

Reedy stopped thinking about the past. "And if you say any of that, Phillips, you're in more trouble than you've ever been." He growled the last, recovering some of his old fire and sputter. I could see where his sons got their taste for fights.

"Sure. I won't say a word. And I hope Dwight recovers fast."

"Thanks," he said automatically. He sighed, a thin scraping sound like the very last leaf of fall skittering across an icy sidewalk. "I hope they put him away long enough to give him some business sense."

"You sure he'd live that long?"

He stared out the window, not even seeing the street. "If he doesn't get any, he won't live long at all." He saw me out.

When I got home there were no notes, no phone calls, no policemen, no criminals. That was lucky. I was too tired to deal with anything harder than a glass of milk.

17

I woke up, or at least got up, early the next morning. I walked into the kitchen, then into the kitchen counter. Marlowe watched interestedly, then stretched and went back to sleep, purring. I hated him.

Tea wasn't going to be enough this morning; I filled the coffeemaker. While I was watching coffee drip into the pot I fell asleep, waking up after my head slipped off my hand and before I hit the counter. I turned on the cold water in the sink and splashed my face, the floor behind me, and Marlowe, who made a resentful noise like leaky air brakes. I nearly fell asleep during that.

After two cups of coffee, though, I could see if I tried, drive if I had to and talk if I'd no other choice. I drove to my office, taking side streets; I still wasn't up to traffic. I thought about Roy's accident on the freeway, then about the way I'd driven the other night, and shuddered.

Once I got to the office I realized that I might as well have stayed in bed, now and forever. Nothing was happening. Rosetti wasn't talking. Rentschler probably didn't know. Elizabeth Grey might not know and probably wouldn't talk. I doubted if Stiff Grey himself were going to walk in and tell where he was, but he was likelier to than Deirdre was just now.

I dialed the hospital and asked about Deirdre Ryan;

a male voice broke in and asked who I was, then said, "Okay, I can tell you. She's still in a coma."

"Is she receiving visitors, officer?"

The voice said disgruntledly, "I coulda been an intern or a male nurse, you know. You can come see her, I think." Muffled voices; he had his hand over the phone. "Yeah, you can come see her."

"Thanks. And interns don't clear visitors—but I'm glad she has protection; don't misunderstand me."

He grunted. "She has a uniformed cop outside her door twenty-four hours. Looks like she's a girl that needs him. She won't be able to say much for a long time."

"I do enough talking for two." Then it hit me. "Unh. I'll be down at one o'clock if that's all right."

"It's fine. You okay? You made some kind of noise back there."

"I'm fine. Just fine. I'm digesting something." I hung up and kept digesting. I really could do enough talking for two if I wanted, and maybe I could convince people I'd done some listening. I looked up Rosetti's home number—still listed under Grey's name—and called him.

I waited several rings for him; he was elderly and took his time. When he answered he didn't sound at all rushed. "Yes? Benito Rosetti speaking." In the background I heard a string quartet playing, probably something by Mozart.

"This is Nathan Phillips. I hope that's a record I hear; maybe I've underestimated you."

"I'm sure you have—but it is a recording. I enjoy music during breakfast. To what do I owe this call?" He was warm, poised, self-controlled. I thought of my own "breakfast," and winced.

"I just wanted to tell you that Deirdre Ryan, whom you may know, woke up today. She's under guard, and she'll be sedated until I go see her at one o'clock. She said she has important news that she won't tell anyone but me."

"Congratulations. I hadn't thought the young lady was so exclusive." That crack took him down a lot in my estimation. "But why are you telling me this? I wouldn't think you'd want me to know."

"I'd like to talk to you afterward. I should be leaving the hospital by one-fifteen; could you meet me in the coffee shop or on the stairs out front?"

"You haven't said which hospital."

"I didn't need to. You know which room, and which side she's sleeping on."

"Perhaps I do." He sounded a bit stiff now.

"Perhaps you do. Do you always keep such careful track of people you sneer at?"

"Be careful, young man. I do have a temper."

"Nice of you to be concerned for my welfare."

"Let's say 'concerned about it.' One-fifteen, on the stairs outside the building. Be prompt. Goodbye, Phillips." He said my last name as though dismissing a butler. I felt dismissed.

I stared at the phone after I'd hung up, then decided it would be wise to keep moving and observable during the next few hours. I went to the public library, the HCR Plaza, Nicollet Mall, and Dayton's. I got a spy thriller, a snack, new gloves, two ties and a case of nerves.

At the hospital I had to show my ID to one uniformed cop and a "nurse" who was packing a sidearm as inconspicuously as possible. I asked the uniformed cop, "Who's paying for this?"

He shrugged. "Depends. If she talks on somebody important, the D.A.'s office will help out. If it's a federal crime, feds might help out."

"And if she dies?"

He brightened. "That makes it even easier. Homicide'd take care of it, then."

"And if none of that happens, and she's no good to anybody?" I wanted to see how far Pederson had committed himself.

He brightened even more. "Maybe somebody'll shoot you." I gave up.

The gun-packing nurse let me into Deirdre's room, looked at me with mixed curiosity and disapproval and went out. I went to the chair by the bed and sat down.

The room was that antiseptic white that goes with aspirin, cotton and hospitals. There was an uncomfortable chair, which I was in, and a bare and cheap night table, which I put my hat on. There was a photo on the wall of some place with beautiful arches, pretty blue tiles and ugly gray walls; the caption said, "Ospedale degli Innocenti." I didn't know what it was doing there.

I sat, shifting in an empty search for comfort, and looked at Deirdre. She was covered in bandages from her stomach up—either she had too many broken ribs or not enough whole collarbone. There were vivid bruises on her eyelids, though the swelling was down; the red marks on her cheeks still hadn't faded. Her head was circled by a strip of gauze, and her hair in back had been shaved off. Her jaw was taped from ear to ear, probably wired as well.

Her eyes were shut, and her hands—several fingers splinted on each hand—were folded across her chest. She looked peaceful and tired and innocent and old all at the same time. She was the prettiest girl I'd seen and the ugliest thing.

I sat and looked at her for a while. I didn't want to stay, didn't want to look at her; I had to stay in the room long enough to make it seem like an interview. I waited.

I couldn't help looking at her. In the muted light from around the Venetian blinds the bruises near her eyes could have been smudged eye shadow, the red, scraped cheeks merely badly rouged. Her mouth, lips puffed, might have been pursed to stifle a yawn. She was a weary young woman back from a very rough night on the town. What she needed was a good-night kiss and her own soft bed. She wouldn't get either.

"Deirdre," I said quietly, "I'm sorry. Sometimes things get rough in my line of work. I guess you found that out for yourself. I didn't mean to put you in harm's way."

She didn't accuse me, didn't pardon me. She just lay there, serene and broken, like a porcelain figure someone else had dropped.

"It isn't like you weren't already in for trouble when I met you," I said defensively. "You mixed in with Rosetti before you met me. You're not in the sweetest business in the world, either. I'd feel worse if it were some shrinking violet or a homecoming queen from Washer High—but you're neither of those. You're a tough girl in a tough business. You're no innocent."

Her small-boned body, her almost-smile sleeping, her folded hands all answered me: No. You're wrong. I was innocent of this, of all this pain and injury, before you came along.

I couldn't argue with that. "All right, maybe you were; maybe we're all still innocent, one way or another. Maybe even Stiff Grey was. What can I do about it?"

She didn't have any more answers than I did. She lay there and didn't move; once in a while her eyelids twitched like she was going to blink.

I'd spent enough time for a believable interview; I got up and pulled on my hat. I turned in the doorway and looked at Deirdre. She looked the same as when I'd come in, maybe a little more tired; she'd had another rough night last night, and she'd go right on having them. No soft bed at home. No good-night kiss.

On an impulse I went back to her, bent over the bed and kissed her lightly on the cheek, on an unbruised spot. "Good night, Deirdre. Sleep as well as you can." She didn't sigh, or speak or make any sign that she felt or heard me. I might as well have been a thousand miles away; maybe I should have been. I guess I wasn't Prince Charming.

On the front steps I scanned quickly from left to right, looking to see Rosetti before I left the shelter of the doorway. He was pretty easy to spot; he hailed me. "Phillips."

I looked around, made sure there were witnesses and said loudly, "Yes, Mr. Rosetti?"

A few heads turned. He laughed and walked up to me. "Don't bother, Phillips. I'm not going to hurt you. You wanted to talk to me?"

I looked past him at the ice forming in the street and at the telephone lines snapping briskly in the wind. "That's right. I wanted to ask you some questions. But you won't be happy with how many answers I already have."

He looked at me searchingly. "Come now. Do you think I'll believe that foolish streetwalker said anything to you?"

"Call her unlucky, and be civil about it. And you don't have to believe it as long as my client does."

"True." He didn't seem upset. "But can you prove anything to your client's satisfaction, from what—" he made a mocking bow "—this young lady under your protection has told you?"

"If my client wants me to, I can use what Miss Ryan said to find proof."

"And what would you find?" The amusement never left his voice. His right hand never left his gun pocket. Such a nice jolly man.

I put my hand in my pocket and tried to look casual but prepared. "I'd find Grey—or what's left of him."

"So," he said, his eyebrows raised and his voice full of laughter. "You think I killed him?"

I hedged, just in case someone else had done the killing and Rosetti was covering up. "I didn't say that," I said in his own lightly mocking tone. "I just said I'd find what's left of him."

I was totally unprepared for Rosetti's reaction. His eyebrows went down and met; his smile faded. "So." There wasn't any laughter in his voice. His hand moved once in his pocket; I froze. He looked around at the people passing by and his hand relaxed.

"Interesting. I'll see you soon, Phillips. And that," he added, looking at me sadly, "will be the final time." He patted me on the shoulder with his left hand, turned and walked away. I was still standing, my hand frozen in my pocket, waiting for his first move.

I went across the street to the florist's. By a hospital there's always a florist's shop; the owner's always fat. I bought a half dozen long-stemmed roses and sent them to Deirdre. I sent them with a signed get-well card; I didn't want her frightened by them if she woke up. I considered sending another half dozen to myself, but decided against it. Too showy. And too soon.

18

I WAS STILL AT THE OFFICE at five that afternoon,
patting myself on the back for getting in control
of the situation and upsetting Rosetti instead of letting him upset me, when the phone rang. I picked
up the receiver and cradled it between head and
shoulder as I reached for my appointment calendar.
"Hello?"

"Mr. Phillips." I almost dropped the appointment
book; somehow my office was instantly smaller,
colder and nastier. "This is Elizabeth Grey. After
reading your first report, I have decided further investigation is futile. Please make up a bill for all
your services so far. Make sure your bill is neat,
readable and extends in detail the itemization you
have already sent me."

A little voice far in the back of my mind whispered tentatively, "I don't know, but I think you've
been had." I gripped the phone numbly and said,
"You're calling it quits?" It sounded dumb, but not
half as dumb as I wanted it to.

"Certainly. I am not a charitable institution for
amateur detectives. You haven't found much, and
your services are far more expensive than I'd expected."

I knew she wasn't charitable and I wasn't an amateur, but that didn't seem important just now. I'd
spent the morning setting up a professional killer;
now I was being told I had nothing to do but sit and

wait for him. "Uh, Mrs. Grey, this is a very bad time to stop the investigation—"

"That isn't my concern. I'm sure you can find other things to do." Like bleed to death on someone's doorstep. "Goodbye, Mr. Phillips."

"No, it's a bad time because the investigation is nearly over." I heard the voice in the back of my mind say, louder and more sure of itself, "Maybe you've been had." I ignored it.

She hesitated. "I just told you it was completely over," she said, but she was listening.

"I mean successfully over." My nose didn't start growing, and my tongue didn't turn black, so I kept going. "Another three days will wind it up. Possibly four, if you want the police—and I have to talk to you about that."

"Go on," she said coldly. She was hooked. "I'm curious to hear what you have to say."

So was I. "Uh, there are some developments you don't know about."

"Yes?"

"I'd rather not go into them over the phone. It's about what happened to your son."

"What is it?" Her voice was sharp and eager.

I finished going out on a limb. "Mrs. Grey, the material is touchy enough so that you'd best come up and hear it for yourself. I can't say it over the phone, and I won't put it in writing. I'll give you the—ah—evidence, and you can write it down, but I don't want any of it in my handwriting or typed on one of my office machines. If you can't do this, we'd better go to the police instead, immediately." Silence. I gripped the phone, wondering if she could hear me sweat.

She bit. "Mr. Phillips, I want this investigation out of the way as soon as possible. I will make immediate arrangements to fly to Minneapolis;

Charles will call you later with my schedule. But you'd better have excellent reasons for forcing me to travel."

"I do. Believe me, Mrs. Grey, I do." She hung up without saying goodbye. She was eager, but never polite. I stood with the phone in my hand, looking blankly at it. Across the room, on the closet door, was a mirror I used to straighten up before important business; I looked into it and listened to the voice say with flat authority, "You've been had." I was watching my lips move.

19

My OFFICE LOOKED JUST AS BLEAK the next Monday morning as it had the previous week and just as empty of facts. Three days of poring over my notes had told me nothing definite. I was certain Grey had disappeared and pretty sure who'd done it and why; I was pretty sure Mrs. Grey was lying to me about something important and certain she was despicable. I also had an idea how Rentschler got on to me so early in the case. But I still needed something awfully persuasive to trot out, and quickly; Mrs. Grey was flying in that afternoon.

I looked up at the calendar across the room; it had a picture of two hunting dogs loping through an autumn field with malice aforethought. It was last October's calendar; Roy had left it up for a joke. He and I always fought about Marlowe's bad habits and how any sensible man would like dogs better. Roy didn't have a dog—he and Edith had never had any pets—but he enjoyed a good joke—or a bad one, for that matter. When I'd cleaned Roy's things out of the office, I hadn't been able to throw that calendar picture away; there was too much of Roy in it.

I stretched out in my chair and thought about Roy Cartley and the relaxed, accustomed way he'd been handling things by the time he'd hired me. Twenty years of practice had made him a careful, unflappable operator. I remembered his advice on a job where too much had happened. "Stay as calm as you can, Nate; try and find the best spot to watch it happen from." Then he said, grinning, "And if nothing happens where you are, sometimes it pays to stir things up. No fun watching something dull."

I looked at the phone and at the pad of phone numbers I'd accumulated over the past few days and at the police printouts I'd started with. I went over the list Grey's mother had given me of checks he had sent her, noting how regularly they had occurred and what the amounts were. Then I called Arizona to get her residence.

Like everybody else, when I was a kid I used to make crank calls: "Is your refrigerator running?" "Yes. . . ." "Go chase it." That was how I felt now; for a while this job was going to be fun.

A woman answered at the Grey establishment. "Elizabeth Grey's residence." She sounded joyless and mechanical; feelingless now, miserable in retrospect.

"Yes. This is Nathan Phillips. Is there anyone there related to Elizabeth Grey?"

That didn't tip her. "Mrs. Grey has no relatives here," she said dully. "And Mrs. Grey herself is gone."

"I know," I said with dignified sadness. "She was to have met me in Minnesota this afternoon."

"Was?" She was beginning to catch on.

I sounded astonished. "You mean the authorities haven't— Oh, dear."

"What authorities?" There was an odd catch in her voice. It sounded like hope; there are some people whose lives are so dreary only a touch of death can put a little life in them.

"I'm very sorry." I sounded as suave as a broker. "I'd best talk to Mrs. Grey's attorney. He'll know what to do."

"Yes, of course," she said breathlessly. I could

almost see her starting to sparkle. "But he's not due at the office for half an hour. He starts at ten, you know."

I looked at my watch, opened my mouth and remembered the time difference. "Of course. Please, call him and tell him to call me in, uh, forty minutes." That gave him thirty to get to the office and ten to have fits. I gave the woman my number. "Thank you very much. By the way, who is this?"

"This is Mrs. Harpf, her housekeeper."

"Her housekeeper. So, you're— Well, well." I didn't need to do a good job of acting; this woman was anxious to fool herself.

"What is it? Had she spoken of me? We were close, you know." She emphasized the "were." I decided never to lie down in Mrs. Harpf's house; she might bury me.

"I'm afraid I can't say. However—" I dropped my voice confidentially "—it's an open secret that I was looking for her next of kin and that the search wasn't going too well."

She gasped. "I'll get in touch with Mr. Jeffers right away," she said faintly. "Thank you very much, Mr. Phillips."

Then she hung up. I sat back in my chair, and she, probably, sprained an ankle hanging crepe. I didn't wonder about her knowing my name; around Elizabeth Grey there would be a constant effort to get in on something worth a slice of cash, by whatever means possible. Thinking of all the effort Mrs. Harpf was putting in, I was almost sorry I wouldn't be worth anything to her.

I underestimated Mr. Jeffers; it was exactly fifty-three minutes later that my phone rang. I let it ring twice; it could use the practice.

It was Jeffers. "Is this Nathan Phillips? For God's sake, man, what's going on? Mrs. Grey's house-

keeper claims you told her Mrs. Grey was dead. I
patched a call through to her plane; she is alive and
well and will be arriving in Denver about now. And
she has a bone to pick with you when she gets to
Minneapolis. She isn't dead, Mr. Phillips." He took
a breath, finally.

"I'm glad to hear that. Really, I don't know how
these things get started. It's a good thing you called,
though; I wanted to ask you about some checks."

"Checks?" he said sharply. "Checks?"

"The ones her son sent her. Some of those sent in
the past few years—of the uncashed ones—" I
crossed my fingers and knocked wood quietly,
"—may have been fraudulent."

He squeaked. He actually squeaked, like a pig being booted through a gate. "Fraudulent? Fraudulent?" Then he quieted down. "I was concerned
when she refused to tell me why she hadn't been
cashing them. But—"

"Please be calm, Mr. Jeffers." I pretended to rifle
through a series of receipts. "I'm concerned only
with one of the checks at the moment. . . . Let me
see, I have a series of checks, coming regularly,
for—"

"One thousand dollars, monthly," he snapped. "I
learned she was withholding them from her regularly scheduled transactions when she brought all of
them in yesterday and asked me to begin cashing
them separately." He sounded pleading. "I had no
previous knowledge of—"

"Oh. Those. All of them are fine." I heard a sigh,
and an intake of breath which might explode in
indignation any second. "The last check—the irreg-
ular one that arrived recently—is the one I'm concerned about."

The intake turned into a sputter, but he didn't
crack yet. I rustled some more papers and said rue-

fully, "Do you know, I can't seem to find my records on that check, and I just noted it yesterday, too."

"You misplaced your records on a ten-thousand-dollar check?" I thought he'd drop on all fours and bark at me.

"Oh. Sorry. Here it is. Payable to Mrs. Elizabeth Grey, the sum of ten thousand and no—"

"I know what a check is." Make that "drop on all fours and bite me." "What evidence do you have to suggest it might be fraudulent?"

"I really can't go into it until I've talked to Mrs. Grey. It would be in confidence, you know." My, but I felt smooth. "However, Mr. Jeffers, let's suppose I had incontrovertible proof that her son did not sign some of those checks."

I stopped in case he wanted to scream. He didn't; either my pitch was weakening or he had run down. "Of course," I continued, "rather than proceed with the investigation, I thought I should contact you right away."

"Of course." He made it sound a little like "Thank God," but I could tell he'd become suspicious of me.

"—And, though it is premature, I have a suggestion to make. Telephone the Minneapolis-St. Paul Security Bank—"

"What?"

"Wait until I'm finished. Warn them that from now on you, as representative of Steven Grey's principal heir, would like the bank to confirm any check over five hundred dollars drawn to his account and bearing his signature. Legally, I'm not so sure you have any right to do that, but if you suggest that you may be investigating, they may extend the courtesy—diplomatically, of course. Suggest nothing about previous checks. But phone them now—be-

fore someone takes away all the money Mrs. Grey
stands to inherit.''

I could hear a soft whistling on the line; I wasn't
sure whether it was from a bad connection or from
all the air leaking out of Jeffers. ''Mr. Phillips, are
you really saying all of those checks are fraudulent?''

''I didn't say the regular checks were,'' I said
crisply. That wasn't a slip he'd make; he knew
something I didn't. ''And since Mrs. Grey stands to
inherit, anyway, it doesn't matter if any of the
checks to her were fraudulent; she wouldn't con-
test it as his heir, and the bank would just as soon
not think about it. After all, they don't want any
trouble, either. The problem is, if someone's writing a bad check or so drawn to Steven Grey, the
same person may write others. That's a large estate,
but no estate can afford to be gutted like that. It
isn't part of my job, but I thought I'd bring it up.'' It
was part of his job—and a profitable part—and we
both knew it. He thanked me and said he'd get right
on it.

The last thing I asked before hanging up was,
''This is the right thing to do, isn't it?''

He dropped into his best courtroom manner and
said with God-given conviction, ''Of course it is; of
course. It is both the easiest path to take and the
best.''

''Oh. Thank you.''

''Don't mention it.'' The further we got from my
suggestion, the more it sounded like it had been his.

When I hung up I laughed like I hadn't in weeks—
not since I'd heard Cartley tell one of his godawful
jokes, in fact. He'd tell you a putrid four-liner as
though he was sure it would roll you on the floor,
and when you didn't react he'd chuckle to himself
and suddenly bark, ''Laugh, goddammit!''

Thinking of Roy doing that made me remember going down to the H & M Grill with him for weekday lunches. I hadn't been there for lunch since the last time I'd gone with him. I went there and ate two BLT's like I used to, and I sat at the counter bothering Ed the cook and trading stories. I told him the rottenest joke Roy had ever told me, some sleeper about a mouse in a Westinghouse refrigerator. Everyone agreed that it stunk; I had a fine time.

20

AFTER A LEISURELY LUNCH I barely had time to get to the airport before the afternoon flight from Denver came in. That was all right; I didn't feel like hurrying. I had to wait for Mrs. Grey, anyway; they helped her off the plane last. I listened to the loudspeakers for more garbled announcements, but nothing good happened. Nothing was funny. I was probably the funniest thing in the terminal; in a few minutes I was going to be a stitch.

"Mr. Phillips, Mr. Nathan Phillips, please come to the defamation booth." That wasn't funny, either, but I went. On my way I passed the monument—nothing but a slab, really—to law-enforcement officers who'd died in the line of duty. I'd never cared much for it before. I thought about Roy and wished his name was on a monument like that. Maybe I'd ask Mrs. Grey to buy him one.

It was all the same as last time. There were the spotless chromed wheelchair and the immaculate attendant. There, too, was Mrs. Grey, looking just as irritable and just as disappointed as she had last time. "Mr. Phillips. After the extraordinary morning you have had, I was not sure you would show up."

"I always keep appointments, ma'am. Besides, all my mornings are like this one was." She stared at me sharply, and one of her withered hands twitched on the chair arm. I looked bright eyed, happy and carefree. She slapped the chair with a ropy forearm and turned to the attendant.

"You may go, Charles. Forty minutes." He nodded, almost turned it into a bow and left. I moved behind the chair and eased her slowly into motion. "Now, Mr. Phillips." Her voice was like very thin ice, cold and ready to crackle. "Please keep me moving the entire time; I need to speak to you."

"No, Mrs. Grey; we're going right back to the spot we talked in before. And I'm doing a good deal of the talking."

She sputtered. She did it literally, with droplets of spittle flying from her mouth. It wasn't pleasant. Nothing about her was pleasant.

I pulled to a stop, wheeled her gently around to face me and pulled a chair up in front of her before she was through percolating angrily.

"Now, Mrs. Grey, are you ready for me to start talking?"

She finally got out, "Haven't you done enough talking for one day, young man?"

"It's like salted peanuts; once I get started I can't stop. Especially when I have such interesting topics."

"You've been more than interesting so far today. On my way here at your request, I received two emergency messages: the first informed me that my housekeeper thought I was dead, the second that my lawyer thought I was financially embarrassed to the sum of ten thousand dollars. Both calls were sparked by your handiwork, Mr. Phillips." She looked at me and waited.

If she expected me to deny anything, I disappointed her. "I was protecting your interest from a bad-check artist, Mrs. Grey—"

"I don't pay you for that."

"Some services you get free. If a little deceit was

involved, I'm sorry, but there's been so much lying
on this case that I didn't feel I was doing my share."
Her right hand twitched as though I'd stuck a pin in
it. "Mrs. Grey, why did you tell me you were not
getting checks from your son when they've been
arriving regularly all along?"

She glared venomously at me. "My financial affairs are none of your damned business."

"Oh, but they are. You got your regular dole
every month from your son, but something was
wrong. Something was very wrong. You said he
stopped sending checks two years ago; what he actually stopped sending was notes with the checks.
So you stopped cashing the checks and held them
for two years, planning what you should do about
your suspicions."

Her fingers moved restlessly and agitatedly. I was
reminded of the toy snakes that come in sectioned
wooden blocks, the way her bony arthritic fingers
writhed joint by joint. Her face tightened with fury
and pain. "My housekeeper told you. I'll destroy
her. I'll take away her salary; I'll cut her from my
will."

"Your housekeeper didn't say a thing. You were
clumsy and obvious; once I knew you were getting
the checks, there was no question how you knew
your son was missing. You also didn't tell me, by the
way, about the ten-thousand-dollar check someone
sent you from your son's account yesterday."

"You had no need to know." The glaring mask
was back, controlled. But her neck had a visible
pulse, and her hands were white with protruding
tendons as she gripped the chair arms. A small child
following her mother turned and stared with terror-
stricken eyes at this strange woman, her lower half
dead and incapable of movement, her upper half
alive and struggling to be still. The girl ran away

and grabbed her mother's hand. I hoped the poor kid wouldn't have nightmares.

"I had every need to know about those checks, Mrs. Grey; it would have made things much easier. Even now it tells me a few things. It tells me that you wrote to your son a few months ago; rather, you wrote whoever was writing checks in his name."

Now she looked amazed. I was still batting a thousand. "And I can pretty well guess what you said. You said you were considering an investigation into your son's disappearance. The checks from Minneapolis didn't get any bigger, so you hired me to shake things up. I did. Some people got shot, some people got beaten up, but I guess that wouldn't bother you.

"You also wrote to Minneapolis when you were starting the investigation. You told the check writer who you were hiring, to make it easy to be sure you weren't lying. That's the only way he could have got on to me so fast. The person you wrote to let some other people know it, just to make my life exciting. Believe me, Mrs. Grey, it did." She looked less than sorry. I went on.

"Then you got this check for ten thousand dollars. You liked that, and it meant you were willing to call me off—just as long as I'd given you enough information to put the squeeze on with, if the checks slacked off again. You needed me in the first place for two reasons: because the police didn't count your son as missing as long as you said his checks were valid—and you were too greedy to destroy them or say anything that might invalidate the checks you were holding—and because you thought that, unlike the police, I could be stopped later."

"Did you speak to the police about my affairs?"

"Not half enough. I had plenty of chance to; this

whole business has had them watching from the start. But I kept my mouth shut and my business private, and I hope I'm never sorrier for anything I do again.''

She wasn't listening; something I'd said earlier had finally sunk in. ''What do you mean, I *thought* you could be stopped?''

I took out my handkerchief and mopped at my face. Pushing her chair would have been less of a sweat. ''I can't afford to drop this case, Mrs. Grey— not anymore. Without violating your confidence, since you'd already telephoned the police to ask them to recommend a private investigator, I told a lieutenant in Homicide what little I could in exchange for more information. He didn't forget what I told him when I got involved in two beatings and a shoot-out; the moment you drop the investigation— which he doesn't want interfered with, for police reasons—he'll find an excuse to haul me in, which shouldn't be hard, and the department will pry everything they can out of our supposedly confidential business. If the lieutenant thinks I did something illegal, and he can prove it, my license goes— and with it, depending on the crime, perhaps your privileged status as a client.''

I stopped for breath. She didn't interrupt me. ''The first thing he'll do then is try to find out why you dropped the search. If he smells blackmail connected with murder, we're both in trouble; not only would we both get stiff sentences, it would totally sink my chances of staying in business even if by some miracle I got acquitted. The publicity wouldn't do you any good, either.

''But let's pretend we could avoid all that somehow. Still, someday the blackmail money will stop coming, and you'll threaten to start investigating again. This time the man that's paying you will decide to scare you; the easiest way is to kill the other person that knows anything about the blackmail. That's me. Since I doubt if you'll call me before making the threat, I won't be ready. I don't want to wait for that. Besides, after what I set in motion yesterday, it might not be a long wait. I'm finishing this case, and you're paying me to.''

She opened and shut her mouth several times. Her jaw popped in and out of place with a muted grinding. "I shall not pay you, and you shall stop."

"Oh, no, Mrs. Grey. I'm going right on, and you're going to pay me. Because the moment you stop, I won't have a thing to keep me from going to Lieutenant Pederson and saying that I suspect you of complicity in the murder of your own son."

"How dare you?" She drew her upper half to its full height, looking like an accused queen. Something in me started burning, then became a flash fire.

"Oh, come off it," I snapped. "You sneered at him, you ignored him except to take his money, you offered to betray him in court, and now you're blackmailing the man we both think killed him. You hired me in hopes I'd prove your son was dead. Why would I think you *wouldn't* kill him?"

"You couldn't." She was looking smaller and less formidable. "You couldn't go to the police."

"I can—and if I do, they'd look into your son's records and notice all these checks you've just started to cash. Then they'd find out—from me— what I suspect those checks were for, why you kept them uncashed for so long and who they were from. Then you'd face a court trial, maybe for blackmail, maybe for accessory after the fact to your son's murder. You'd be acquitted of the first charge, probably, and almost certainly you'd get the second thrown out of court even if they find the body. Just the same, for some time you'd be set up, and mocked and forced to stay in what you call 'this wretched climate,' unless you could get a change of venue to Arizona—which I doubt. And the newspapers would have more fun with you than a dog has with an old rag doll. My, but everyone would sneer at you."

The thought of people sneering hurt the mother as much as it had hurt her son. She was shaking, and I thought for a moment she'd cry. I thought I might cry for her myself someday, when I had nothing better to do. I sat and watched her, waiting for her to regain her self-control.

When she stopped shaking I said quietly, "So I assume I'm still working for you. I'll report regularly. It's not a total loss; this way you'll get your son's estate whole, instead of plundered by his killer, the check forger."

"They were not forged checks." Her voice was so calm, so nearly serene, that I couldn't believe it was hers. "I've had experts look at them."

I stared. Now I understood why the lawyer hadn't had a stroke when I'd hinted the regular checks might be forged. "That I'll admit is news to me, Mrs. Grey. I did know, though, that the police had their own experts look at checks drawn to the same account, and they didn't come up with anything. The police weren't entirely inside the law to do that. I hope you're not shocked. Tell me: would your son have been foolish enough to sign blank checks two years in advance?"

She sniffed. "Steven was foolish enough to leave money lying out on his desk at home."

"How much did you net?" She ignored me. "Never mind. I'll call you if anything important turns up." She glared at me. I stepped behind her chair, as much to get out of her sight as to roll her away.

Even though we were fifteen minutes early, Charles was there. Maybe he could read minds. He nodded to Mrs. Grey and then, just barely, to me; I turned the chair around and he stood behind it, waiting. He was in a good line of work for waiting. Everyone around Elizabeth Grey was waiting for something—death, or ruin or further orders.

She signaled to Charles to start rolling, then made a stopping motion and looked me in the eye. If her son stared like she did, I could understand his nickname.

"One question, Mr. Phillips. What on earth made you think of blackmailing me for a crime I did not commit?"

Charles's eyes widened, but he said nothing. I smiled. I'd been hoping she'd ask that. "It's nothing new, really. I once saw a vice-squad man do it to shake down a cheap hooker."

Charles almost lost his composure and his job at the same time. He launched into a coughing fit and managed to roll Mrs, Grey along so rapidly she didn't dare turn and look at him.

21

When I got home Marlowe strolled out of the shrubbery and yowled at me. One of his ears was torn at the top, and he had a large scratch alongside his jaw. When I took him up and put antiseptic on him, he wouldn't let me rub his back or tickle his chin on the unhurt side.

"Don't be so proud, cat," I pointed out as I swabbed his torn ear. "I was pretty tough today myself."

The phone rang. I finished what I was doing, then picked it up. "Nathan Phillips speaking."

"Took you long enough to get it. You oughta learn to answer your phone."

I drew back from the receiver, then remembered that breath couldn't come in over the wires. "I'm a slow learner. Hi, Greasy. What's up?"

"You know those two guys I told you about? The ones I been looking for?"

"Yeah?"

"I saw one of them today."

"That's good." Like hell. "Did you get his name?"

"No." It was a strange "no," one that might have been "yes" if I'd been there in person to keep him from lying. "I sort of hoped you'd know their names."

He didn't keep up with news too well, in all probability; I wanted to make sure he was lying.

"Find anything to tie them to Deirdre Ryan's beating?"

"Yeah," he said uncertainly. And then more confidently, "Yeah. I talked to them girls on Hennepin Avenue, and they said it was them all right. The two I saw today."

"You said you saw one." So much for my reliable, skilled operative.

There was an uncomfortable silence. "Uh...the other guy was with him."

"What do you want me to do about it, Greasy?" I said nastily. "You know one guy now; for all I care you can ask him the other guy's name. I'll be on the lookout for them, but you're in a better position to find them, and you've done one hell of a lot of nothing for me yet."

"Maybe I will ask him." Greasy sounded hurt. He slammed the phone down with a bang, several times, finally hitting the phone cradle. Another dissatisfied customer. Maybe I needed a PR man.

Funny; I thought I needed a hot bath and the rest of the afternoon off a lot more. I skipped the PR man and took the afternoon off and the bath. I soaked in the tub for a long time, basking in the hot water and in the warm feeling that someday soon I'd collect a fat fee from a client who hated me.

At ten o'clock the next morning my phone rang. Marlowe was walking back and forth on my chest, telling me to do something about it. I rolled over and picked up the phone. Marlowe didn't like that. He leaped off and sat on the other side of the bed, looking injured and rubbing his head with one paw; he wasn't feeling any too good this morning, either.

"Unh." I wasn't at my wittiest.

"Phillips?" It was Pederson.

"Unh?"

"Are you all right?"

"Unh."

"Did I wake you up?"

"Not yet." I sat up, using the phone and my other hand to cradle and lift my head. I leaned on the rest of the phone accidentally. "Why'd you phone me? I didn't put in for a wake-up call."

"I'm not room service, either. Stop fiddling with the phone dial, will you? You keep dinging in my ear."

"I thought that was my ear. What's up?"

"Nothing much. A friend of yours has disappeared."

I was awake. I pushed the window curtain partway aside and looked out. Snow. Lots of it. "Are you going to tell me who, or not?"

"You're a real sweetheart when you wake up, aren't you? Greasy Joe is gone."

"Joe Heinicke?"

"If you say so. I never remember his last name. His landlady called the station last night, madder than hell. He rented a furnished room yesterday afternoon, sold the furniture by nightfall and bought a bus ticket out of town. He left behind most of what he owned—a clean dirty shirt, a pair of beat-up shoes, some other garbage—and just scraped up cash and disappeared."

"Where did he go?"

"His ticket was for Chicago."

I didn't like the way he said that. I didn't want to say so yet. "How do you know?"

"First, we found a bus schedule in his shirt pocket."

"Found it on him?"

He sounded hurt. "What a suspicious mind you have. It was in his room, in the shirt pocket. So tell me: why did you think he'd still be here—think he'd be dead?"

I said, "I didn't say that," but went ahead and told him about Rentschler's thugs, Joe's promise to help find them, and his phone call last night.

Pederson commented, "I'd think he was dead, too," ignoring my denial.

"Then why say he's skipped town?"

"Did I say he'd skipped town?"

I could hear my alarm clock humming to itself and outside the wind driving snowflakes against the window. Marlowe stalked over and rubbed against my back. I needed it. "Get to the point. Did he skip town or didn't he?"

"You tell me." Pederson was half serious. "Like I said, we found a bus schedule. At the station they remembered his buying a ticket to Chicago. He wasn't on the bus when it got to Chicago. We had him for theft, so the Chicago cops met the bus; no luck. After that we checked again at the Greyhound station on this end. Nobody saw him down there when the Chi-town bus left—and two custodians remembered having seen him around earlier, but not then. People keep an eye on Joe; must be the snappy way he dresses. Anyway, it seems he bought the ticket but never got around to using it."

"Anybody seen him since?"

"Not unless you have." Not quite a question.

I scratched my head. "I don't know where he is or even where he might be. Have you checked off all the bridges, and are there any new bodies in the river?"

"Quit kidding. If we checked every body of water in the Cities, we'd use up the Department funds for this year—and we'd probably find ten bodies, none of them his. We'll look for him in the spring harvest, if he hasn't turned up before then." Late in most springs, on principle and on suspicion, the combined agencies of Minneapolis, St. Paul, and Hennepin and Ramsey counties drag various bodies of water, including parts of the Mississippi, and compare notes. They always turn up a few people—people who had taken a Brody, people who had bad friends or none at all, boozers, addicts, bad drivers.

"So you won't know till then where he went, if he doesn't turn up anyplace else."

Pederson said, "Hell, he's only a derelict. If it weren't for his involvement in the Grey investigation, nobody'd care."

My ears must have come to a point; Marlowe backed off and regarded me dubiously. I tickled his ears with my free hand. "My investigation, or is there something I don't know about?"

"Let's just say an investigation could start, especially if Greasy doesn't turn up or turns up dead. The more we hear about you, these days, the more likely it is to start. By the way, what's your guess on Greasy?"

"I don't know. He could have upset Rentschler's thugs." I hesitated, but didn't dare not say it. "Pretty dumb of him to leave the schedule lying around like that. Anyone could find out where he'd gone, with luck."

"Yeah," Pederson said flatly. "I'm glad to hear you say so. Just wanted to make sure you weren't helping him put one over on somebody."

"Who? Me? Never. Maybe Greasy put it over by himself, though I doubt it. He'd have trouble outsmarting your average fireplug."

Pederson chuckled. "From all I've heard, that's true. Keep me posted." He said goodbye and hung up, leaving me to think.

I got dressed and headed for the office. It was snowing still, and we'd had a couple of inches already. As usual in spring, the snow-removal bud-

get was overdrawn; the city let snow pile up as long
as it could, then cleared the main roads first.

I slid quietly up First Avenue, trying to avoid the
few cars illegally parked in the street—whether the
plows are out or not, cars are supposed to be out of
their way, and every driver knows the city never
runs out of money for parking tickets. Between
skids I tried to think. I had plenty of time; I couldn't
do more than ten or twelve miles an hour.

Joe's behavior puzzled me. Either he was desperate to leave—and dumber than even he looked—or
he wanted people to think he'd left, but he was
really staying—which was dumber still. Maybe he'd
bought a ticket for one place and gone another, but
I doubted it. Right now that sounded awfully smart.
I was wishing I'd been that smart, myself.

Finding a parking place downtown was a lot easier
than getting into it; I had three car lengths and it
still took me four tries. All the while, thick wet
flakes piled up on my windshield; the wipers just
pushed them into clumps. The wind had come up;
damp as the snow was, it started drifting. From the
looks of things, I wouldn't see much business that
morning.

22

I saw no business at all. In the rest of the morning and most of the afternoon I got two calls. One was from a husband with an advanced case of cabin fever, demanding to know if his wife was running around. I told him I wasn't sure yet and wanted to know more facts; to make the research easy, his wife got on the line. They yelled at me and at each other for a while, then dropped me out. I don't think they noticed when I hung up.

The other call was from a man who offered me the princely sum of five dollars to drive all the way out to Coon Rapids and back with some overdue library books. I laughed at him but not nastily; he really thought I'd be well repaid for my time. I offered him six to deliver a pizza to my office. He got the idea and hung up.

I expected more of the same when my phone rang at three o'clock. I answered with my automatic name-and-company routine.

The caller was brief. "Phillips?"

I recognized the voice. So soft, so gentle sounding; like it belonged to a florist, not a killer. "Speaking." Barely. "Rosetti?"

"Couldn't you respect my age and call me Mr. Rosetti?" A sigh. "Oh, well. Not that it matters anymore. You've been very foolish. I'm sorry, Phillips. You're so young." There was a click.

It was just as well; I didn't have a thing to say. It

wasn't like him not to say goodbye; I suspected he
was saving it to say in person. I stood up, paced the
office, checked the chambers of my .38 to make
sure they were all loaded and generally fidgeted.
Why now? What made him decide so suddenly if the
other day hadn't?

On an impulse I called the Minneapolis-St. Paul
Security Bank. The staff were still there, in spite of
the storm; when someone answered I only said, "I
need to talk to the Junior Subchief of Programming
in Accounting."

"Which one?"

"There's more than one? The one I talked to made
it sound exclusive. I mean the guy with the almost
beard, the guy who sounds like Harvard and looks
like the tooth fairy."

That got a laugh. "I know him. Right away."

"Right away" took five minutes, while I counted
bullets and checked the window across the street
for rifle barrels. I didn't think anyone could shoot
me from across the street in this weather, and I was
just arguing with myself about standing between
the window and the light when someone came on
the phone. I ducked from surprise.

"Junior Subchief." The voice was crisp, clear,
confident and just annoyed enough to sound pa-
tient.

"Hello, Junior." I was not in the mood for manners. "Remember me? I'm the guy who turned out
to be an exception and cashed a check for one dollar
from an old lady."

He caught his breath. He remembered, and he had
a reason to want not to. "What do you want?"

"I want to know—"

"Please don't come to me saying that."

"—the answer to one question: what are your instructions and the tellers', if I call or come in?"

"I couldn't tell you that. That would go against policy," he said faintly.

"How do you know? Did someone specifically say it did?"

"No. But it stands to reason."

"The bank president himself gave you instructions to see to my needs once. Wouldn't you bet I'm still an exception?"

"Not in this case."

"In other words, whatever instructions you have came from him."

"You said it; I won't deny it." There was a soft sound; maybe he licked his lips nervously.

"Damn nice of you not to deny it. If you won't tell me anything, will you connect me with Mr. Williams?"

"I'm sorry, Mr. Phillips, but that's against policy, too."

"Wish you hadn't said my name out loud. Don't you ever worry that you're being asked to do something unethical or even illegal by your employer?"

"My superior has legal responsibility for all actions, initiating at this office or above, following policy. As for being unethical—" He stopped, then said shakily, "I refuse to discuss it. I try to leave my ethics at home when I come to work."

"Don't ever bring them; it doesn't sound like they'd stand the strain. Now, connect me with Dawson Williams. I was an exception once, and I will be again."

"I doubt it." His self-assurance was back. "Why should I let you talk with him, if he probably doesn't want to be bothered with you?"

"Because," I said flatly, "you could get in more trouble for not letting me talk than you could for letting me, if you did turn out to be wrong."

He had to untangle that. When he did he said unhappily, "All right. Since you're so insistent, I'll put your call through. God, I will be so happy to get back to my machines!"

"Who knows? Maybe they'll be as happy to see you; there's no accounting for tastes."

He sniffed and put me on hold. I waited with no patience at all.

Williams sounded impatient, too. "Hello? Who is this?" I identified myself. "Well, Mr. Phillips, I hardly expected to hear from you again."

"I guessed you didn't. That's why I pulled an end run around your secretaries."

"You needn't expect me to congratulate you."

"I expect you to tell me what's going on."

"Then you expect too much."

"I don't think so. Not from a man who is condoning a check fraud."

"Don't bother threatening me." He was triumphant. "Tomorrow you won't be investigating this anymore, I imagine. Or much else."

"Then you might as well tell me what's going on." I was beginning to understand why Stiff the Snow Man might take his business to this bank.

"All right." He wanted to gloat. "Yesterday we received a phone call from out of state—"

"Arizona."

"Yes, as a matter of fact—warning us about possible fraud in the Grey checking account. Naturally, we were quite alarmed; we thought your investigation had turned up concrete evidence. Furthermore, the call came immediately following a large check drawn to that account—"

"To the tune of ten thousand dollars and sent to Arizona."

"My, but you've done your homework." The gloating wasn't going well. "To go on: we belatedly took your advice and, today, refused to cash any more checks on that account for Mr. Rosetti. When he discovered we were serious he was—upset." He paused.

"I can imagine. Any mortal wounds?"

"Nothing like that at all," Williams answered testily. "He just came in to talk to me and argued that we should cash the check. He was, er, very persuasive."

"He can be. He frequently persuades people who don't want to die to do so, anyway."

Williams said lightly, "I cashed his check for him. Unfortunately, he was still dissatisfied."

"What did he want—interest? A toaster?"

Williams cleared his throat. "No. He wanted to know who had suggested the surveillance on Grey's account."

"And you told him."

"Of course." Unembarrassed, calm, annoyingly secure.

"Mr. Williams, you promised to respect my confidence. I did respect yours."

"I imagine you did, but only to the letter. A poor sort of honesty."

"Have you seen enough honesty to judge?"

"I'm very sorry, Mr. Phillips—"

"I'm going to be gunned down," I said wonderingly, "and you're sorry."

"It was a question of policy, that's all."

"'Policy' seems to mean you do what you want, whether it's legal and moral or not."

"Be fair. We do what seems expedient."

"I don't feel that fair, Mr. Williams. What else did you promise Rosetti?"

"We agreed to contact him if you called, wrote or stopped in again."

"God, you're considerate. Should I call him now for you?"

"That won't be necessary, Mr. Phillips. The gentleman you talked to a moment ago has telephoned him already, I feel sure."

I thought about that. " 'The gentleman' doesn't approve of your business ethics, you know."

"I know. It doesn't matter; he does as I tell him."

"Good. Maybe I'll see you both in jail." He was saying something about policy as I slammed the phone down.

I stared at my desk for a while, then got up and put on my stocking cap. As soon as I did the phone rang. I put it against my ear and said "hello," then rolled up my cap on the receiver side and tried again.

It was Pederson. "I said 'hello' back, Phillips. Bit early in the day to be drinking, isn't it?"

"Not today. What's up?"

"I thought you might want to know. A man named Alvy Louis got beat all to hell this afternoon."

"I don't have time to get flowers; just put my name on the card. Who's Louis?"

"Funny, I thought you'd know him. He's a thug for Reedy Rentschler, and he's the best-dressed thug in town." After about ten seconds he purred, "You all right, Phillips?"

No. "Yeah."

"You wouldn't know anything about it, would you? It's kind of important; Louis might die."

"What happened to him?"

"You don't want to know; it's pretty bad."

"Broken arm?"

He didn't say anything for a moment. Then he sighed. "All right, what do you know?"

"I don't know a thing. I can guess that Greasy Joe didn't skip town. What happened?"

"A couple of old folks from Bemidji were driving

by Minnehaha Park, watching the snowstorm. You wouldn't think people from Bemidji would like snow that much. Anyway, the wife looked out the window and said, 'George, there's a man out there,' and George couldn't see well because of the snow, and said, 'No, dear, it's just a big dog, but it's limping; one of its front paws must be hurt.' So he got out to help, only he was wrong. It was a man.''

He left time for me to say something clever. There wasn't anything.

"The man's lips were all curled back in pain till they looked like a snarling animal's; his eyes didn't see anything. His right arm was just hanging and flopped like it didn't have any bones at all. One ankle bent the wrong way. He kept saying, 'I'm cold,' over and over, probably because there was a big bloody hole on top of his head, and there was snow in it. They got him to the hospital; if he survives the shock, the exposure and the injuries, he'll be crippled. He'd better try a new profession, too; this one didn't seem to work out.''

"Yeah." I took a deep breath. "Did they see anyone else around there?"

"No."

"Any buses by there at that hour? Did they see any taxis?"

"No buses; I doubt it on the taxis. What—"

"The guy that did it got away somehow, and Louis got there somehow, too. Any abandoned cars on Hiawatha or on the Parkway?"

Pederson swore three times quickly. "I should have thought of that. I was too busy getting ready to nail you for information.''

"Serves you right. Find out the year and make of Louis's car, and the plates—"

"And if we can locate the car, we'll probably find

Greasy. Okay, okay, I'm no moron. What are you going to do?''

"I may call back. I think I'm going to collect some life insurance." I hung up.

Then I called Rentschler's office. "Mrs. Rentschler, this is the man you want to kill. Could I—"

"Which one?"

"Phillips. Could you—"

"Oh, that one."

"Stop being cute, I've got to talk to Reedy. Alvy's been beat up."

"You're yelling."

"Sorry." I liked her a lot better angry.

"We heard about Alvy, anyway. Where'd you hear?"

"That's what I have to talk to Reedy about."

It took no time at all, this time. "Phillips? If this is another of your goddamn cute tricks to get through to me, I swear I'll nail you to a wall somewhere."

"It's no trick, and there's no time to fool around. You heard Alvy got beat up pretty badly this afternoon?"

"Sure." It sounded deadpan, like the click of a safety on a small gun.

"Well, he isn't the only one scheduled to get it. I want to stop the attacker before he gets me in trouble with the police and messes up my investigation."

"That's damn nice of you. Why the hell didn't you stop him sooner?"

I wasn't the one who started him, but why bring that up? "I didn't know sooner. Tell me: what's the name of the guy that works with Alvy? I mean the guy with the gold tooth and the Fort Knox tiepin."

Total silence. Then: "Why tell you?"

"Because the attacker who beat up Alvy is doing Alvy's sidekick in next, and if you don't get me

there to talk the guy out of it, you'll have to kill him
to stop him." I held my breath, waiting to see if it
would take.

"We might want him dead," Rentschler grated.

I knew then that I'd won. "Not a chance. You're
too much the businessman. There's already been an
assault the police are investigating; any more violence will be tied to you right away. If I go, and
something goes wrong, there'll be less of a connection to your business."

I heard a scrabbling, then the loud crunch of antacid tablets being chewed. "All right. Iver Norgaard," and he gave me an address on University
Avenue, right by Dinkytown.

I wrote it down. "Alvy and Ivy? You'd never
think it to look at them. Call Norgaard and tell him
I'm coming, so he doesn't shoot me on the way in if
his other friend hasn't shown up yet. Don't be surprised if he can't answer."

"Right." More tablets crunched. "But if you're
wrong or lying, Phillips, you're dead." He hung up.

I pulled my hat back down and threw my coat on
going out the door. I barely remembered to check
for men hiding around corners on my way downstairs.

23

AT LEAST I didn't have traffic problems; 35W was amazingly empty for four-thirty on a weeknight. A lot of employers must have closed up early because of the storm; the people I saw were the last cautious stragglers of rush hour. I was as cautious as they were. The road was covered with a dirty brown-and-white slush that was packing into solid ice.

I rolled carefully onto the stretch of 94 that joins the two halves of 35. A ways ahead of me on 35 was the approach ramp where Roy Cartley was killed, smashed into a spin by a drunk who merged at sixty without looking. I didn't have time to think much about it and probably didn't need to; I wasn't in any great danger of dying by accident just then.

Even the university was shut down, at least partially. The West Campus complex was barely visible through the snow; there were few lights on. I turned north, back on 35 now, and continued across the river.

I exited onto University Avenue but stopped at the intersection and stared ahead, brooding. If I didn't turn, I'd plow straight ahead over University, past 4th Street and back onto 35 within three or four car lengths of the place where Roy had died. Funny—if Roy had driven up here, he'd be alive; if I went back down to where he died, I'd stand a better chance myself. I turned right, onto University.

The houses in Norgaard's neighborhood were occupied mostly by fraternities, religious groups and students. Norgaard lived between the Xi Phi Alphas and a health-food co-op. It was an odd address for a gangster; he must have liked noisy neighborhoods and college kids. I wondered if he'd liked Stiff Grey.

Pulling into the neighboring drive, I shut my motor off and rolled to a silent stop. Before I got out I pulled my stocking cap up and stretched it out of shape, then took out my .38 and slid it under the cap, muzzle forward. I was glad I liked a small gun and stretchy caps.

I took a pocket flashlight from my glove compartment, held Kleenex over the bulb end to dim it and checked the cars around me. All of them had university stickers in the back windows, barely visible through the snow. I walked quietly over to Norgaard's driveway.

That was better. The Firebird in the drive didn't have a sticker, but the tire tracks behind it showed it hadn't been there long. It was registered to A.V. Louis, 1624-something; the street name curved out of sight upside down on the steering column. I didn't need it. I went up to the house's front door and tried the handle gently. It was locked. I rang the doorbell and ran around to the back.

I didn't have much time and needed more than I had; the back door had a Yale lock—a job for experts with time on their hands. So I pulled on it, kicked it, heaved my shoulder against it and tore back to the front door.

It was unlocked now. I ran in, looking around and hanging on to my cap.

Greasy Joe stepped out of the front closet. He cradled a tire iron in his sling and held a gun the size of a drainpipe in his other hand. It looked like a .44, beat up but effective. "What in the hell are you doing?"

I raised both hands, then put them on my hat. The gun was still there; I hoped it didn't show. "Trick or treat."

He pointed the gun at me and repeated his question, savoring every word slowly and clearly but absently at the same time. His gaze was commanding and unwavering, but his pupils had shrunk to little pinpricks of darkness. I didn't like his eyes at all, but this looked like a bad time to tell him that.

I held very still. "You weren't giving me any information, Joe." My voice was plaintive. "You never told me a thing. I had to find out everything for myself. Finally you disappeared, and I had to find you to ask what's going on."

It sounded silly even as I said it. I had to remind myself that the concentrated alertness in Joe's manner had nothing to do with intelligence. He stared at me aloofly and waved the gun. "Back up."

I did. He waved the gun some more. I kept backing and he kept waving till I was flat against the front wall. He reached into his sling and took the tire iron between his palm and the gun. He turned with unexpected speed and said into the closet, "Come out," poking quickly with the rod and gun.

The man that stumbled out had a gold tooth and a gold tiepin. His tie was torn; his plain clothes looked rumpled and even plainer. His face was solid, unequivocal fear. He looked at me. "Do something," he croaked.

That gave me my cue, but I hated like hell to do it to him. I tried to look relaxed without taking my hands down. "Why should I? Greasy and I had a deal. He's got the guys he wanted now. He said he was taking them to jail; if he changed his mind, well—" I shrugged. "I don't work for the law. I only came to make sure Greasy wasn't in trouble. Why should I help you?"

Greasy looked my way briefly, without taking the gun off Norgaard, and nodded. "I hoped you'd see it that way." He added with just a trace of his former amiability, "Young fella, you might not want to stay for this. I'm messed up and happy, and I'm gonna take my time making this guy sorry he ever met me."

I didn't think Norgaard could turn whiter, but he did. Nobody's ever looked sorrier.

"Wait a minute." I got Greasy's attention, but the gun stayed on Norgaard. I tried to sound panicky. "Maybe you'd better not take your time, Joe. I think I was followed here."

That got him. "By who?"

"Whom."

"Don't get mouthy. Who followed you?"

"I'm not sure. Maybe a cop. Maybe another of Rentschler's men. You'd better hurry." My hands were still up.

He turned to Norgaard. "Kneel down." Norgaard knelt down, helpless with fear, and looked at him. "Now hold your arm out."

Norgaard started to cry. "No—please, please don't—" His cheeks wobbled.

The tire iron swung into line with his face. "Your arm or your eye?"

"Oh, Jesus," Norgaard whispered. He put his face in his hands and sobbed. There was nothing I could do; Greasy was still turned partway toward me.

"The arm." His voice was commanding, implacable. Norgaard got in control of himself and stretched his right arm out straight, his eyes closed, sweat-beads all over his face.

Greasy smiled and raised the iron over his head.

I yelled, "The window!" and fired the .38 at the glass. I'd raised the gun off my head, but even so it was deafening. I saw the windowpane shatter but didn't hear the falling glass. I saw Greasy turn, drop the tire iron and fire methodically five times through the window. He braced his wrist on his cast; I saw the gun kick back and shake his entire body but didn't hear any shots.

As he started firing I threw myself behind the chair next to him, as if ducking. I got my balance and jumped behind him, spiking the back of his knee with my heel; he whirled as he went down, trying to point the gun at me. I kicked his hand as hard as a star soccer goalie would boot a near-miss. The gun spun out of his hand and fired into the ceiling; I still couldn't hear anything but ringing.

He leaned forward to grab the gun as it came down, and I rammed my knee into his jaw. My knee stung, but he went over backward on his left side and lay limp. I pointed my gun at him and nudged his good arm with my toe; the arm stayed limp.

I turned to watch Norgaard stumble to his feet. It took him three tries; his knees wouldn't hold him. He turned to me and tried to say something. "Save your breath," I panted. "I can't hear a thing."

He nodded, wobbled a little, then got steadier. Suddenly he dove for Greasy's gun, picked it up and whirled toward me in a crouch. He pulled the trigger. I didn't hear anything, but this time I wouldn't have, anyway.

I shook my head. "Can't you count?" My voice sounded muffled and far away, but I could hear it— bone conduction, probably. My fist caught Norgaard on the chin; he was still staring at the gun in disbelief. My hit staggered him, and he straightened in time for my next blow to catch him on the breastbone. Weakened as he was, he went down and stayed there. I held my own gun on him and rolled him over; he didn't move. "Teach you to be ungrateful." I was panting harder.

I lurched to the table, pulled a lamp off it and tied Norgaard's hands together with the cord. I used the extension cord from the same lamp to tie Greasy's right arm to his right leg. If he could reach behind himself with his broken arm and not pass out untying himself, he deserved to get away.

I picked up the phone, dialed the police and asked for Pederson.

"Pederson here." He was tired and irritable.

"Talk louder. Rough day?"

"Dammit, Phillips, I had my hat on to go."

"Then we're even from before. How would you like to send someone to a house on University Avenue?"

"Why me? Is it homicide?"

"Will be if Louis dies."

"You've got Greasy Joe, then." He sounded relieved; I wondered if it was because I was alive or because I hadn't killed anyone. "Norgaard's okay, too, then?"

"You catch on fast. They're both tied up in Norgaard's house, at—"

"I have the address in front of me. I didn't know this was your day to collect for us."

"Sure—twice a week, odd days of the month. Now, could you send someone, fast? I can't stay to come in."

"You can stay, and you will." Then he added more reasonably, "Look, you've had enough trouble for one day without our giving you some, too. Promise me you'll stay until the police come."

"But I—"

"Promise."

"I have to—"

"Promise." There was an edge in his voice.

"All right. I'll stay till the police get here."

"That's what I like to hear." He said goodbye and

hung up. I redialed immediately; I didn't have much time. I still had the numbers I needed scrunched up in one coat pocket, but this one I nearly had memorized.

"Hello."

"Mr. Rosetti? I'm glad you're home; this is Nathan Phillips." I tried to sound scared; it wasn't hard. "What I want to say is, I just phoned the bank president. I think we ought to talk."

"Isn't it a little late for that, Phillips?"

"No. Really, we can reach an agreement; I guess I wasn't thinking before."

"You weren't." He was amused.

"So could you meet me at my apartment at about eight o'clock?"

"Could you make it any later?"

"Sure, if you want." I put all the eagerness I could in my voice. "I'm not at home right now; I'll be there about ten to eight."

He chuckled. "Well, I suppose I should be more tolerant of the young. Eight-thirty, then."

"Thank you, sir."

"You're most welcome. Good evening." He waited for me to say goodbye before he hung up. In his case, somehow, good manners didn't count for much—and I didn't miss the fact that he hadn't said "goodbye." Not yet.

Quickly I looked at my crumpled paper and dialed the other number on it. Mrs. Rentschler answered. "Hello?"

"Phillips here. Norgaard's okay; put Reedy on."

She set the phone down. It was our shortest conversation, easily our best. Reedy got on immediately. "Phillips. How's Norgaard?"

"Fine. I stopped Greasy. Norgaard has a sore jaw, but otherwise he's all right."

"I guess I underestimated you, Phillips. If you

drop by anytime, I'll have a little something for you that you'll like.''

"I can't drop by tonight, Reedy; the police are coming for Joe and Norgaard, and I have to wait till—''

He made a strangling sound and grated, "I overestimated you, Phillips. Drop by anytime; I'll have a little something for you that you won't like.''

"What caliber?'' No reply. "I can't drop by after I'm done with the police, either. I'm going to be at Rosetti's house, and we'll be talking from 8:30 to about 9:30. If you want to send a man by to see me then, you can—but I might not need to talk to you then.''

Silence. "Better get the antacid tablets out,'' I said softly. "Your stomach's going to hurt a lot soon.''

That got him. "What's all this got to do with me?'' he said finally.

"Rosetti's noticed that someone's been moving in on Grey's business. Let's just say your name could come up tonight.''

"I'll send a man by. You want him to pick you up at Rosetti's?''

"Why not?'' I was the life of the party tonight. "I'll be glad to see him.''

"Sure.'' Rentschler sounded uncertain. "Well, goodbye, Phillips.''

I slammed the phone down as the police pulled up in front. I made sure the front door was unlocked, then ran out the back. I'd kept my promise—and in the best Pederson style. I left the back door open.

I leaped the hedge in between Norgaard's home and the frat house, and slammed the fraternity's back door, hard. I edged along the back of the house, where a drift would hide my footprints from the frat house's doorway; then I walked down the other side of the house to the driveway and my car.

As I pulled out with my lights off, I could see the police running across to pound on the frat-house door. I drove as quietly as possible till I was half a block away.

24

I DROVE SLOWLY AND CAREFULLY down the interstate; I couldn't see very well with all the snow on my windshield, and I didn't want to wipe any off. I peered out the side window and crawled down the road; I had plenty of time if I had any.

It wasn't six yet when I parked half a block from Rosetti's place—no use calling it "Grey's place" anymore. I got out and closed the door gently. There were about two inches of snow sloped up on the windshield; to all appearances my car had been there at least half an hour.

Getting back in the car half an hour later, carrying four tacos and a cup of coffee from the local Mexican franchise outfit, was a lot harder. The door wouldn't latch without my pulling it sharply. Most of the snow stayed on the door; I settled down to wait, thinking and eating tacos. Except for the streetlights coming on, nothing had changed while I'd been gone.

There was one bad moment around seven-thirty; a cop came along and gave me a parking ticket. I ducked way down under the dash, but I shouldn't have bothered. The windshield was almost totally covered, and the cop stuffed the ticket under the wipers without so much as peering inside for the registration. I had a wild urge to sneak around the front fender and rip up the ticket. Other than that there was no excitement; it was cold, dull and uncomfortable.

Not quite ten minutes after the policeman passed, Benny Rosetti came out his front door, looked both ways carefully, then put his back to the street and locked the door. He walked casually down the street, his right hand in his coat pocket. Once he looked back at his home—there was a light shining from nearly every window—then looked up. It had quit snowing, but clouds were still moving rapidly across the city-lit sky. An occasional searchlight flickered across them.

He moved down the block to his car. There didn't seem to be a ticket on it—funny. He drove off slowly in the snow-filled street, turning south at the first corner.

I didn't get up right away; if Rosetti had second thoughts and came back, I'd rather not be where he'd find me. I leaned back in the seat and tried to visualize what he was doing.

In five or ten minutes, depending on how cautious he was behind the wheel, he'd turn west on a road that would turn into Lake Street. Probably he'd continue on it past Lake of the Isles, right down to Nicollet and then down that till he could turn on 33rd and go to First Avenue, and my apartment. All of this would take him anywhere from another ten minutes to twenty.

There was a spot on the west side of First that would give him a clear view of the front and back of my apartment, and he'd still be able to watch north and south for approaching cars. I was sure he'd park there, but it didn't matter; wherever he parked, he'd wait there once he saw that my lights were off. I hadn't left the reading lamp on this time; this morning I hadn't known I'd need to.

By eight-thirty he'd probably get restless. It wouldn't be like me to be late for an appointment at my own home, not an appointment I'd all but begged for. He'd stare up at my window, wondering if I were trying to trap him. He might try sneaking upstairs, but I doubted it; a professional killer as old as he was would never be that reckless.

Any way I figured it, he wouldn't be back before nine. With luck the wind wouldn't die down, and it would take him another twenty minutes to drive home. I should have plenty of time if I started around eight. I sat and watched, checking to see if any more lights came on in Rosetti's place. None did; it was a safe bet that all lights left on were left on purpose by Rosetti. Every minute it got harder to wait.

At five minutes to eight I couldn't take it any longer. I was cold, out of tacos and coffee, and nervous; I'd counted my bullets five times to make sure I'd replaced the one I'd fired at Norgaard's house. Another five minutes and I'd probably shoot myself in the foot to make sure my gun was working.

I got out of the car, brushed the snow off the windows in case I needed to leave in a hurry and went up to the front door. I'd timed it pretty closely; Rentschler would probably send someone around to try and pick me off on the way to my supposed conference- at Rosetti's house. I looked around but didn't see anybody. I rang the doorbell, just to be on the safe side; I could always say I was lost. It wouldn't be far from the truth, either.

Nobody answered. I waited, glanced up to see if anyone had come to the windows and tried again. After three minutes I reached into my inside coat pocket and brought out a small packet. The smallest pick, the one with the loop end, did the job. I stepped in, closing the door behind me. No burglar alarms went off; Rosetti didn't want the police investigating any break-ins.

There was a stairwell in the back, neatly glassed

in and separated from the rest of the house. I went
directly upstairs.

Unfortunately, for a house one person lived in, it
was spacious; there were three floors and a base-
ment. I checked the second floor at a trot, then
went over it again slowly. Main bedroom, nothing.
Chances were, if this were Rosetti's bedroom, then
taking Deirdre upstairs meant upstairs from here. If
whatever she had seen was still here it would
probably be on the third floor. Even so, I thought
I'd make sure. I checked in the linen closet, looked
in the drawers of the walnut bureau. I checked for
niches behind the curtains. There was a window
seat with a velvet cushion; I took the cushion off
and checked there.

All that I turned up were linen, shirts, curtain-
pulls and a dusty copy of *National Geographic* with
an American Indian on the cover. No bodies. No
coffins. No dubious-looking bags or boxes.

On the way out I had a gruesome thought and
went back to check under the bed. There was hardly even any dust.

The other rooms were much the same: neat, ex-
pensively but tastefully furnished, well cleaned and
disappointing. Supposedly Rosetti did his own
housekeeping. That meant he was good at two
things.

In one room there was a rolltop desk with a black
leather swivel chair in front of it. In another room
was a glass-fronted bookcase full of antiquated edi-
tions in excellent shape. In the last room on that
floor was a small grand piano with a tattered book
of Scarlatti sonatas open on it. In none of the rooms
was a body.

The bathroom, except for a large tub with clawed
legs, was surprisingly modest. Rosetti was an old-
world gentleman; apparently, he didn't believe in

fancy plumbing. There weren't any marble counters or gold fittings. What's more, there wasn't any place to hide large dead things.

That brought me to the third floor. I was getting pretty sick of Rosetti's closets, wardrobes, hampers and knickknack niches, and I was running out of time. Even so, I didn't skip anything.

I didn't need to; the upstairs was only four rooms. The rooms were large, though. The first one, in back, was a guest bedroom, bigger than the master bedroom. There was a four-poster in the middle of it, with brocade pull curtains and a heavy canopy stretched over oak ribs. I looked under the bed, then patted the mattress for a cut-out middle, then stood on it in my stocking feet and tapped the canopy to see if anything were up there. No luck.

The rest of the room was over furnished but under equipped with hiding places. The closet in the outside corner was empty except for three wire hangers and a baited mousetrap. There were no other closets; a rectangular projection in the inside corner showed where someone had built into the room for the neighboring room's closet. Poor planning.

The room next door, toward the front of the building, was Rosetti's library. You had to go through the guest bedroom to get there. Whoever had built the upstairs hadn't worried about that any more than they had about putting in a bathroom; I supposed Rosetti didn't have many guests. In the library, oak shelves lined every wall. They were the deep kind, large and grainy and with maybe a foot of wasted space behind the books. I pulled books out every three feet, bracing myself for a grinning face without much face left peering out from the holes. Then I went back around, tapping the backs of the bookcases for hollow spots, feeling more like

a kid playing Sherlock Holmes than I did like a
grown-up. No hollow places. I got so absorbed I
nearly bumped into the bend where the adjoining
room's closet was built out into this room. I tapped
around there pretty carefully; all I found was a
splinter.

One knuckle bleeding, I checked the display case
in the center of the room. There was a skull in it,
but it was a monkey's—either a souvenir of a safari
or Rosetti's idea of something pretty. The case was
full of small animal skeletons, neatly mounted,
numbered and labeled. As I left for the next room,
my mind kept wandering back to those neat little
cubes of steak and the mangling Rosetti had given
them. Everything in the house reflected his neat-
ness mania. Where was the violence?

At the door to the other front room I stopped.

There was another rectangular cut out of the
room, exactly like the ones in the bedroom and the
library. There wasn't a door in the cutout. Three
places for closets. One room left.

I could see the last room in my mind: two closet
doors, one on each inside wall at the inside corner.
Both closets coming back till they almost touched, a
set of shelves in the back of each to confuse anyone
who tried to judge their depth. Between the two
closets, behind the bookshelves after all, would be a
space about a foot and a half wide—enough to store
a man upright. I thought of Rosetti's delicacy and
patience and of the case with all the mounted ani-
mals—of Rosetti, looking at that case and worrying
about how to dispose of a body while everyone was
watching him.

I heard shots in the street and ran to the window
to look out. A man in a trench coat and black leather driving gloves was shooting from behind a car at
someone in a dark gray overcoat. The man in the

overcoat was sprawled on the sidewalk behind a fireplug. He had his hand in his coat, but he hadn't pulled anything out and he didn't look particularly worried. It was Rosetti.

The shots stopped, and the man behind the car raised his head cautiously, then stood up to peer at Rosetti. It was a bad move. Rosetti whipped his arm up smoothly and relaxedly and fired once. His gun crashed and echoed; it sounded like a backfire if you weren't looking. The standing man staggered, clutching at his shoulder, and dropped to his knees. He swung his car door open quickly; it shut slowly as he disappeared from view inside the car. His hand reached up and turned the ignition, and the car sped away blindly as Rosetti fired again.

Rosetti stood up, brushed himself off as he walked to his front step and disappeared from my sight. I turned and looked for a phone, thinking of dialing; there wasn't time.

Somewhere far below me a door slammed and the lock clicked into place. A quiet, gentle voice said with warm amusement, "Hello, Phillips."

25

I TIPTOED TO THE STAIRWELL, carrying an ashtray. I peered over the railing and waited. Soon I heard the faintest creak of a door on the floor below me; I don't know how he got that far without my hearing him. I dropped the ashtray, as carefully as if I were dropping clothespins in a bottle.

It sailed down two flights and smashed on the banister. The sound it made was a lot softer than Rosetti's gun was a second later; he leaped to the railing like a panther, shooting down. I leaned over, shot him in the shoulder and yelled, "Freeze!" in my best police voice.

He didn't freeze. He didn't show any pain. He didn't even drop his gun; he turned around and sent a shot past my right ear just as I pulled back. My second shot didn't come anywhere near him, but his second took a piece out of the railing I'd been leaning on when I ducked.

"Amateur hour!" he yelled gleefully as he charged up the stairs, chuckling. I wasn't laughing at all. I was running out of the stairwell, my head as low as possible.

I sprinted through the three rooms I'd searched and hid behind the door of the fourth and last room. I noticed there was only one door to the closet and that the walls bulged out exactly as they had in the other four rooms, but I didn't have time to think what that meant. I had an idea of how to fool Rosetti. It was crazy and trite and wouldn't fool a performing seal, and I'd be dead if it didn't fool him. I heard him run up the door and stop, panting.

"Phillips?" he said softly.

I took a chance. "Yes?" I said, my head stuck out by the door panel. I jerked it back as three slugs tore through the door, two where my eyes should have been and one right between them. They were big slugs.

I held my breath and waited. After an expectant pause he spoke again. "Bad, Phillips," he said gently. "Very bad. You forgot to fake falling to the floor. I'm disappointed in you."

"So give me a C-minus." It didn't sound funny to me, but he liked it. He chuckled again.

"Oh, no, Phillips," he laughed. "Oh, no. C-minus is a passing grade. You're not going to pass at all." Funny.

"I thought you only used a .22."

"That's only for formal occasions. This is informal. No fancy invitation. Strictly come-as-you-are."

"I don't suppose you'd take my regrets, anyway." There wasn't much point in talking, but I didn't feel like dying just yet, either.

"That makes it a formal occasion." I heard him fumble in his pocket; then I heard the soft click of a safety on a small gun. It was hard to hear; I'd never have caught it if I hadn't been trying so hard not to.

"Phillips," he said again, barely louder than the gun. "I feel sorry for you, amateur. I'm going to hand my big gun to you, the .45. You can use it and shoot at me when I open the door. I'll still get you first, you know. I'm passing the gun through now. It won't give you much of a chance, but you'll be better off than you are now."

So I looked that dumb—it was nice to know. "Pass

it through slowly,'' I said, and opened the door a crack. The gun poked through—the muzzle and just enough of the rest so that I might have tried to reach for it.

Instead I struck down on it, hard, with my own gun. The .45 fell to the floor, and the .22 behind made a short hard snap as a bullet plopped into the davenport across the room. He'd needed the door open for the smaller bullets. I slammed the door and picked up Rosetti's big gun. It was a thick, flat automatic; I shoved it in my breast pocket, muzzle down. I knew without checking that it was empty. Rosetti was no fool. I held the door and called out, ''Rosetti!''

''Yes,'' he said softly, gently, in his kindest voice. He waited for me to speak. I shifted the automatic in my breast pocket until it was right over my heart, the butt sticking above my heart. ''Go ahead, Phillips,'' he purred.

''What about that shoulder?'' I said, too loudly. I wedged the gun in place with my handkerchief.

''Not too bright of you to bring it up. It hurts some.'' He added absently, ''Makes my head ache. Do you have to shout?''

''Sorry.'' I quieted down. I needed him calm. ''Want to end it?''

''Yes, but I didn't think you would.'' He chuckled. Tonight was a laugh riot.

I took my tie off, knotted one end and looped it around the doorknob and stepped back, holding the other end of the tie with my free hand. ''I'll be ready for you, and you know it.''

''No,'' he said, as though correcting a small child. ''You'll never be ready for me, and you know it.'' There was something to that.

When the doorknob turned slowly and the latch was barely free of the lock, I tugged on the tie and let it go. The door swung quietly open, and a surprised Benny Rosetti stood staring at me, a target pistol in his hand.

My gun was down. So was his. When he saw that he smiled sadly. "Just like the Old West. You're so young." He nodded affectionately at me. "Goodbye, Phillips."

Holding my body as still as I could, I brought my gun up quickly, ignoring his gun as it flashed up and fired twice. I felt the thud of lead against the gun in my breast pocket.

He was just beginning to look surprised when I shot him in the chest. Then he looked really astonished. He dropped to his knees and began the long, slow fall to the floor.

He never made it. He leaped up again and jerked his gun up. I skipped aside as he fired, and put another bullet in his chest. He jerked back, clawed at his chest as he started going down again, steadied himself on his knees, then snarled and raised his gun again. I would have thought he was pulling the same trick I was, but there was blood on his coat, and a narrow stream of it running down his front.

I went over to the closet door and pulled back the dead bolt three-quarters of the way up the door frame. I heard a soft sigh behind me and dropped sideways. His gun went off once; the bullet hit at chest height on the door. I turned and fired at his forehead. Compared to the .22, even my .38 sounded like a cannon. His eyes glazed and he fired twice more, practice shots at nothing in particular. Then he laid his head down and closed his eyes.

I waited twenty or thirty seconds, just watching him, before I walked over and checked his pulse at his neck. He was really dead this time, the original Man Who Wasn't There. I said, "Mr. Rosetti, you weren't kidding when you implied that you

wouldn't be killed easily." My voice sounded high
and foolish. He didn't move or respond; I was glad.

I took the .45 out of my breast pocket. There were
two small slugs flattened against the gun butt, par-
allel to the floor and an inch apart. He couldn't
have been more accurate on a calm Sunday evening
at a pistol range. I waited a moment more, watching
him even though I knew he was dead. If I'd had a
stake to drive through his heart, I'd have used it.

I heard a sound from the closet, a sound I couldn't
place. It was a sort of low clucking, like a worried
hen. I cocked my gun on its last bullet and walked
to the door. I grabbed the doorknob and jerked on
it, ready to slam the door if I had to. I stopped the
door half open and gave a quick look inside. The
doorknob swung free of my hand. The door drifted
silently around and hit against the wall, banging it a
number of times. I didn't count. I wasn't paying attention.

He was wearing a torn, dirty white shirt with
short sleeves. Through tears in it I could see great
mounds of fat, doughy, muscleless flesh, cross-
stitched with thin white scars. His eyes were dark
little holes, surrounded with the puffy black bruises
of numberless beatings. He looked at me vaguely
and spread his pudgy fingers at me, then put his
hands over his head and giggled, waiting to be hit. I
stared.

After a while he quit giggling and shuffled his
way to the middle of his dusty windowless room. He
sat at a splintered unvarnished table, fumbling at
the pile of check blanks on it. He began to write,
slowly and carefully, on one check after another.

Behind him I could see a cot, bolted to the floor,
and a toilet with no seat. The standpipe ran up the
bare wall from the bathroom below; looped around
the bottom of the pipe were a length of rusted chain

and a pair of dusty handcuffs. They weren't needed anymore.

I walked in and looked over his shoulder. He didn't seem to mind, just continued carefully inscribing: Steven Grey. Steven Grey. Steven Grey.

"Steven," I said. It came out as a hoarse whisper. He went on writing. "Steven Grey," I said, a little louder. He looked at the blank checks, then at me, then turned and tore off another check. "Grey!" I yelled, shaking his shoulder.

He didn't answer, just covered his face with his arms and giggled again—a high, meaningless sound without humor, going on and on. I waved my hand in front of his face, but when he peeked out and saw my hand the giggling got louder. Much louder than that and it would have been sobbing.

I gave up on him and walked back into the other room. He followed as far as the doorway, stopped giggling and started clucking again. Rosetti's body didn't mean much to him; neither did anything else.

I thought about pumping my remaining bullet into Rosetti's corpse. Instead I walked over to the window, trying to keep an eye on Rosetti and on Grey at the same time. I looked out cautiously. The street was deserted except for one man, in a dark coat and dark hat, waiting under the streetlight opposite Grey's house. The window I looked through was covered with long barbarous icicles; the man outside seemed to cross behind them again and again, like the shadow of a blackbird.

I moved back from the window, walked over to Grey, took him by the elbow and led him to a chair. He stared uneasily, and the clucking sounded unhappier. He hadn't been out into this room in years, and he knew he wasn't supposed to be. He sat and waited for something to happen to him. I went downstairs, found the phone—at last—and dialed Jon Pederson's office.

"Jon?" I said softly.

"Speaking. Who the hell is this, and how the hell did you know I'd be here now?"

"You nearly always are there. Jon, this is Nate. I'm at Grey's place. I found Grey. He's alive—sort of—and Rosetti is dead—I think."

Pederson sounded unhappy. "Nathan Phillips, one-handed hero. Why call the cops at all? Why don't you just tuck one of them under each arm and carry them over here?"

"Maybe I would, but there's this nasty man outside, and he's got a gun. He ties in to either Reedy or Arnie Rentschler, but I don't want to go outside and ask him which."

"Sit tight," he said immediately. "We'll be there inside of ten minutes, Nate."

I thought of Rosetti lying upstairs. "Could you make it five?" My throat was dry, and my lips felt thick and rubbery, like they hadn't been used in years.

Pederson chuckled—not too nastily—and hung up. I went back upstairs and looked at Rosetti and then at Grey, at the nothing that wasn't there and the nothing that was. The snow men.

The car made it in seven minutes. Pederson was in it. I was sixty by the time they came up the stairs, and by the time they got to the room I was dying of old age.

26

THE WRAP-UP WAS NEITHER SHORT nor sweet except
for the part directly related to Grey, which took
even longer and was even more bitter. During the
next month or so a lot happened. Greasy drew a
healthy sentence for assaulting Louis and Norgaard.
Alvy Louis, with a permanent limp and a twenty-
percent disability in his right arm, got off easier.
Norgaard drew one sentence for extortion and a
stiffer one for assault; Alvy, to everyone's surprise,
testified against him in three other beatings. So
much for the perfect partnership. Reedy, of course,
got left out of it entirely.

Neither Arnie nor Dwight got tried for beating
Deirdre Ryan. I couldn't identify them as her assail-
ants, and when she came out of her coma she either
couldn't or wouldn't. After all she went through
and I went through, she never gave testimony on so
much as jaywalking.

Under pressure she said she'd had a dream about
being taken upstairs by a gangster to meet an incredibly scarred and feeble man, but she insisted it
was just a dream. Probably she was still scared of
Rosetti, even though he was dead. I couldn't blame
her.

I saw her while she was saying she couldn't testify, just after she woke up; I visited her a couple of
times after that at the hospital, but it wasn't much
use going to see her. I was awkward, and she was

embarrassed. When she got out quite a while later, she was back on the street in three weeks, wearing elastic bandages on her ribs and a wig to hide her shaved spot till it grew out. You can't keep a good whore up.

The man outside Grey's house when the cops came was Arnie Rentschler. He blamed me for his brother's wounding, and his father had set him on to me at Grey's house—nobody could prove that last. Arnie also blamed his father, Swenumson and in some obscure way Dwight himself; about then he ran out of blames. Blameless Arnie got sent up for five to ten on Swenumson's testimony; the kid panicked and figured he'd sell Arnie before Arnie sold him.

There was something to that; Arnie listed every job Swenumson had ever done for him, and every other crime he thought we'd believe Swenumson had done. By the end of the accusations it seemed odd that killing President Kennedy wasn't on the list. Arnie probably would have put it on if the kid hadn't been one year old in sixty-three. Swenumson got five short concurrent sentences, and got off easy at that. The judge said he was so young. I flinched.

Surprisingly, Arnie also had concrete evidence against Grey in the Dumont murder. God knows how he got it, but it was his desire to find Grey and pressure him that had caused his and Dwight's first contact with Rosetti, also the real break with their father. The D.A. immediately and automatically went through the appropriate machinery; all it really led to was a pre-trial hearing to judge Stiff Grey's present competence to stand trial.

Elizabeth Grey came up for the hearing, a straitlaced and morally upright mother come to pass judgment on the bad end of a wicked son. That's the way the newspapers played it; they, at least, loved it.

The hearing was hell. Doctors testified that Grey had probably been beaten agonizingly every day for nearly two years. His scars were permanent, his physical disabilities obvious, his insanity unquestionable. The only two portions of his body that escaped extensive scarring were his right hand and his eyes. There was damage around his eyes, and he could barely focus, but he had enough eyesight left to write checks, and he had a hand for holding a pen, and that's all Rosetti wanted left of him.

Most prominent among the injuries the doctors listed was a fractured skull, badly healed, dating from about two years ago. Probably it was the initial wound, after which Grey woke up woozy and in permanent custody.

Perhaps it was Grey's one triumph in a life of disappointments: even Rosetti had been afraid to take him on face to face.

The list of minor injuries went on and on. One of the doctors testifying said flatly that Grey did not have a single rib that hadn't been broken or an internal organ that hadn't sustained damage. Anyone could see what had happened to Grey's teeth and ears; apparently it was a miracle of sorts that Grey was alive at all.

Among Rosetti's effects, it turned out, were a stethoscope, a sphygmomanometer or sphygmometer, whatever—the thing that measures blood pressure—a massive quantity of syringes, and enough antibiotics to keep even Typhoid Mary from spreading infection. Rosetti also had kept a diary tucked in the back of his home medical guide; when he wasn't beating Grey he'd been healing Grey. I suppose that way Rosetti could assess the damage he was inflicting and minimize his chances of losing

Grey. I always thought medicine was a selfless profession.

It was pretty clear to everyone involved that Rosetti had used Grey as an ingenious but not very sane solution to a number of problems: how to hold together a drug organization and avoid gunfire; how to keep Grey an apparent presence without making him an actual one; and how to find release for Rosetti's apparently boundless desire to inflict pain.

Several speculations, all irrelevant, were offered for Rosetti's behavior; one related it to his incredible physical stamina. The theory threw the word "hysterical" in too loosely. The doctors threw it about in whispers until they were all a little hysterical themselves, and the court, tired of the noise and unconcerned with their theories, threw them out.

In his summation Grey's court-appointed counsel pointed out that Grey for two years had been the sole victim of a man with a long record for violence and brutality. The lawyer added, "About the best we can say for the situation is that for two years it kept Mr. Rosetti off the streets." Nobody laughed. It didn't matter much; by that time everyone in the courtroom was sure of the ruling.

Through all this Grey sat in an old suit that hadn't fit him in years and never would again, now. He picked at his sleeve and giggled and flinched whenever anyone came within striking range. Everybody in the room was pretty sick about it except for Elizabeth Grey. She just sat there looking old and unbending and unhealthy and proud. After the hearing's conclusion she petitioned, successfully, to be appointed to care for Stiff and his funds. She took care of the medical proceedings, signed every paper anyone would let her, then dumped her son off and went back to Arizona, where she gloated over her son's money until she died of a stroke eight months later. I hope she was satisfied.

They put Stiff Grey in a private-care facility and tried to educate him for a few weeks. It was hopeless. The only thing he could do was write his name all over everything in sight. After a while the doctors gave up and did their best to keep Stiff comfortable, if not happy. One warm day a year later he lost the rest of his mind, or else found a little of it, and cut his throat on a broken mirror before anyone could get to him. Everyone at the private-care facility was relieved.

My shooting of Rosetti was termed self-defense. Nobody asked what I was doing in Grey's house; I had said we were planning to meet that night, and everyone assumed I had been invited. Some days you get the breaks.

As soon as the police got hold of Rosetti's gun, they let it be generally known what they'd found and shipped it over to ballistics to wait for the rush. The gun was a twenty-year-old Colt Woodsman; its age alone made it sound promising. Sure enough, bullets and requests for tests poured in from cities all over the United States. Within two weeks Rosetti was tied to fourteen killings, with a promise of more to come.

The press picked up on the "Marksman Killer" (I don't know who thinks up these things) and made a big deal out of how tough he was, how fast he was and how incredibly good I must be to have shot him. I felt like the Man Who Shot Liberty Valance.

My life picked up; the publicity brought in a lot of business. I had it made as a solo operator after that; I got used to working alone, people got used to hiring me and that was that.

Jon and I see a lot of each other these days; by the time I'd told him everything about the Grey

case we were both in the habit of talking. When
Dave Komarek and I finally held that bachelor party
for Bernie, Jon came along, swore at us all and called
us irresponsible young rowdies, drank us under the
table and left at dawn. The next day I felt like a victim of internal firebombing and Jon's wife, Willa,
wouldn't speak to me, but Jon wanted to know
when we were doing it again.

Jon went with me one Friday afternoon to the
Minneapolis-St. Paul Security Bank, where we
bored the bank president and scared hell out of the
Junior Subchief. It was more for fun than for jus-
tice; there was nothing we could do to them except
possibly bounce checks. The Junior Subchief swore
it wasn't any of his doing, and besides, he was looking for a new job. I saw him in the bank window the
last time I passed there.

Twice I've dreamed I'm back in that room with
Rosetti. Both times I've made a pot of tea and
stayed up the rest of the night.

The Best of
HUGH GARNER

Now Get These *PaperJacks* Best Sellers!

Available at bookstores or mail this coupon.

FREE!!
BOOKS BY MAIL
CATALOGUE

BOOKS BY MAIL will share with you our current bestselling books as well as hard to find specialty titles in areas that will match your interests. You will be updated on what's new in books at no cost to you. Just fill in the coupon below and discover the convenience of having books delivered to your home.

BOOKS BY MAIL
320 Steelcase Road E.,
Markham, Ontario L3R 2M1

Please send Books By Mail catalogue to:

Name_____
(please print)

Address_____

City_____

Prov._____ Postal Code _____

(BBM1)